THE
ACCOUNTANT'S
APPRENTICE

DENNIS M. CLAUSEN

BROWN POSEY PRESS

an imprint of Sunbury Press, Inc.
Mechanicsburg, PA USA

an imprint of Sunbury Press, Inc.
Mechanicsburg, PA USA

For information about special discounts for bulk purchases, please contact Sunbury Press Orders Dept. at (855) 338-8359 or orders@sunburypress.com.

To request one of our authors for speaking engagements or book signings, please contact Sunbury Press Publicity Dept. at publicity@sunburypress.com.

ISBN: 978-1-62006-091-9 (Trade paperback)

Library of Congress Control Number: 2018958590

FIRST BROWN POSEY PRESS EDITION: September 2018

Product of the United States of America
0 1 1 2 3 5 8 13 21 34 55

Set in Bookman Old Style
Designed by Crystal Devine
Cover by Riaan Wilmans
Edited by Janice Rhayem

Continue the Enlightenment!

CHAPTER ONE

An unexpected knock on the door. A last-minute decision to cross the street. The extra thirty seconds it takes to stop and tie a shoelace. Life turns on the simplest decisions, and suddenly everything changes. Like the Rubik's Cube I keep in my apartment as a paperweight, one simple twist sets countless other hidden forces into motion. A new life, a death, a chance meeting with someone—every motion in the universe is counterbalanced somewhere else. It might not even be on this planet. It might be on the other side of some distant constellation in the darkest recesses of space. Whenever we comfort or ignore the least among us, we change the universe—and nothing is ever the same again.

. . .

My own knock on the door occurred one morning while I was reading a book in my small studio apartment near Downtown San Diego. The walls and ceiling of the apartment were stained from the cigarette smoke of previous occupants who had lived there. Some, I had been told, even died there. Other walls were water stained from toilets or sinks that had overflowed from the second floor. A small bed with a deeply indented mattress and a dark-stained oak nightstand were in one corner, near the door. A small bookcase was wedged into another corner. Some previous renter had dumped the bookcase on the curbside next to several large garbage cans. I managed to salvage the concrete blocks and deeply stained pine boards only minutes before the garbage truck rounded the corner and pulled up to the curb. One of the pine boards had apparently extended too far out into the street. It still bore the rubber imprint of a tire tread from an automobile that had run over it.

A long ten- or twelve-foot radiator pipe jutted out from the ceiling of the apartment, ran the length of the wall, and connected to the radiator on the floor. The radiator was an ancient relic, seemingly rescued from an earlier century. Old layers of silver aluminum paint had peeled away from the radiator's surface, revealing several rusted metal seams. When the radiator was functioning, it moaned and gurgled and occasionally belched steam out of a small, metal vent on the side. Fortunately, the apartment manager only turned the radiator system on during extremely cold winter evenings. Otherwise, I would probably have spent every night lying awake looking at the ceiling and waiting for the next belch of steam to interrupt my futile attempts to sleep.

At first, I thought the knock must have come from the door on the other side of the hallway. No one had visited me since I moved into my apartment several months earlier. So I continued to read my book on the lives of the great men and women in world history and had just started the chapter on some of the world's great saints, when I heard the knock again.

This time it was obviously my door.

I thought about ignoring it. I had been living alone for so long that I figured anyone standing on the other side of the door must be a solicitor or someone else I had no good reason to meet. After a few more persistent knocks, however, my curiosity got the better of me. I placed the book facedown on the end table next to my reading chair and walked over to the door. As it swung open, I was greeted by a muscular, heavy-set man with a crew cut. In his tight-fitting sports jacket, he looked like an ex-Marine who had recently retired and taken up some other profession.

"Yes?" I asked.

"Detective Robert Tindal, San Diego Police Department," he said, holding out his badge. "Are you Justin Moore?"

I nodded somewhat apprehensively, not knowing why a police officer would suddenly show up at my apartment door.

"I wonder if I could ask you a couple of questions about your neighbor across the hall."

"The old man who had a heart attack and drowned in his bathtub?" I asked.

"No. The one who moved in after he died."

"I didn't know someone else moved in."

He raised a huge, muscular arm and gestured toward the interior of my apartment. "Mind if I come in and ask you a few questions?"

"Yes. Of course."

I opened the door wider, and he strode quickly into the apartment. He paused briefly to survey the contents of the room. Then he walked over to my reading chair and sat down. He glanced briefly at the front cover of the book on the end table. Then he pulled out a notebook and pen. I sat down on the edge of the bed on the other side of the room.

"Did you see anything out of the ordinary after your new neighbor moved in?" he asked.

"I told you, I didn't know someone else had rented the apartment after that old man died."

He looked at me suspiciously, as though he didn't believe what I was telling him. Then he jotted a few notes in his notebook.

"I stay to myself over here," I explained. "I don't mingle with the people in this building. I like it that way."

"Well, two people who rented that apartment died rather suddenly. One of them was murdered."

"Someone was murdered over there?" I exclaimed.

The concern must have been evident in my tone of voice because he studied my eyes, seemingly to determine if I was feigning surprise.

"No, he was murdered in Balboa Park. You sure you never saw him coming or going into his apartment?"

"What did he look like?"

"Young man about twenty-five years old. Short hair, very thin. We think it was a drug deal gone bad. But when two people who rented the same apartment both die within days of one another, and one of them is murdered, well . . ."

"When did this happen?"

"Two days ago. Why?"

"About four, maybe five days ago, I was asleep when there was a sound in the hallway. It woke me up. Then there was a quiet knock on my door. I didn't open it because it was late, and, well, some of the people who live here . . . they're a little scary." I paused to collect my thoughts. "I heard someone out there slide something under my door. I waited until I heard the footsteps retreat down the hallway. Then I turned on the light. There was a dollar bill lying on the carpet."

"A dollar bill?"

"Yes. Someone slid it under the door. I still have it."

I retrieved the dollar bill from the top of my bookcase and handed it to him. He briefly examined the dollar bill and placed it in his coat pocket.

"This was probably a warning," he said. "A drug dealer sending notice to your neighbor to pay up or else."

"Why do you say that?" I asked.

"Drug dealers send messages like this. This one most likely got his apartment numbers mixed up. Put it under your door instead of your neighbor's. You're mighty lucky. If you had opened that door, I would probably be investigating a murder in this apartment."

• • •

The next morning I left my apartment and started my daily jog over to Balboa Park. I followed my usual route down Sixth Avenue to the Laurel Street Bridge. As I was about to cross the old, 1915-era bridge that spanned Highway 163, I glanced to my right and spotted several police officers and detectives walking across an area that was marked off with yellow tape. A homeless man, dressed in sweat-stained clothing and carrying a green garbage bag, stood just outside the taped area. He watched the officers and detectives walk methodically back and forth, heads down, staring at the grass. A tall eucalyptus tree with a huge trunk and shiny, light-gray bark was located in the middle of the area marked off with yellow tape.

I paused for a few seconds to watch the search. Then I jogged across the Laurel Street Bridge, under the West Gate entrance to Balboa Park, and past the California Tower and the Museum of Man. I continued jogging until I approached the big fountain near the Natural History Museum. I spotted a food cart on the other side of the fountain and jogged over to it. As I ordered a cup of coffee from the vendor, I spotted a stack of newspapers just inside the area behind the open window of the food cart. I purchased one of the newspapers and walked over to a nearby park bench and sat down.

As I sipped on the coffee, I paged through the newspaper. I glanced at the headline, "Drug cartels spread through region." Another article was titled, "Corporate downsizing continues." On the back page of the "Local Section," I noticed an article, "New Art Exhibition to Open," and another titled "Area Homeless Attacked." On the same page, I spotted the article I was looking for under the title, "Man Slain in Balboa Park." The brief article read, "The body of a man was discovered Tuesday morning in Balboa Park, the apparent victim of a homicide. The victim was discovered by park employees on their morning rounds. Police have not revealed the identity of the victim." The article went on to describe the efforts of the San Diego Police Department to piece together the victim's activities prior to the night he was murdered in Balboa Park.

I gazed into the distance for a moment, pondering what I had just read. Then I pulled a pen and notebook out of my shirt pocket and began writing down some of the job openings listed in the "Help Wanted" section of the newspaper.

. . .

Later that morning, as I jogged across the Laurel Street Bridge again, I glanced to my left and saw that the police officers and detectives were wrapping up their work behind the yellow tape. The homeless man I had noticed earlier was sitting on one of the huge exposed roots of an imported Moreton Bay fig tree closer to where I was jogging. The exposed roots of the fig tree rose several feet above the ground on both sides of the homeless man, making it look like he was sitting in some primitive jungle setting in what was otherwise a manicured and neatly mowed park. Our eyes met briefly as I jogged past the area where he was sitting. As I turned south on Sixth Avenue, I glanced back at him again. He was still staring at me.

When I walked into the front door of my apartment building, I paused briefly to check my mailbox in the foyer. I flipped through the junk mail as I walked down the hallway to my apartment. As I inserted the key into the lock, I heard a muffled noise in the apartment on the other side of the hall. Turning, I saw that the door was slightly ajar. When I nudged it open a few inches to peer inside, Detective Tindal suddenly stepped out of an adjacent kitchen and looked in my direction.

"Need something?" he asked.

"No. I heard a noise."

"Ever been in here before," he asked suspiciously.

"No."

He nodded not very convincingly and continued to eye me suspiciously. Then he looked around the apartment as though he was seeing it for the first time.

"I'm checking it out before I give the manager the okay to rent it again," he explained. "There's really nothing here. Doesn't even look like he ever really moved in."

"Do you know who he is?" I asked.

"Well, we have a name. Whether it's his real name . . . that I don't know. My guess is whoever he was working for planned to set up some kind of a drug operation that involved this apartment. Most likely gave your manager a fictitious name."

"I saw an article in the paper this morning about the drug cartels operating in this area."

"Ya, this city's going to hell in a hand basket," Tindal replied angrily, as though he took the criminal activities in his town very personally. "Can't escape from it. It's everywhere."

As I turned to leave, he stopped me in my tracks.

"Wait!" he said. "I have a few more questions I need to ask you."

"About what?"

"I did a background check on you."

"And what did you find?"

"There are some things we need to talk about," he said in a tone of voice that reminded me of the way movie detectives talk when they interrogate a suspect they are certain is guilty of a crime. "I learned that you are an ex-priest. And you were involved in another murder in San Diego."

"I was the *witness* to a murder, if that is what you mean?"

"Yes, that's what I meant. Can you tell me about it?" he insisted, still eyeing me suspiciously.

"I'm sure you have a record of it in the police files."

"I just wanted to hear what happened . . . in your own words."

"I was counseling a woman who was having marital problems, when her husband suddenly burst into the rectory. He fired a bullet into her head. Then he ran out of the rectory and disappeared."

"Do you know why he didn't kill you, too?"

"He looked at me and seemed to fixate on my collar. I told the police I thought he just didn't want to kill a priest."

"Is that why you left the priesthood?"

"I didn't *leave* the priesthood," I corrected him. "I was given a leave of absence to sort out my emotions and feelings about what happened that day."

"Did you?"

"Did I *what*?"

"Sort out your feelings about what happened that day."

I hesitated and then replied none too convincingly.

"I'm working on it," I said.

"So that's why you're in hiding? No telephone. No computer. No car. No forwarding address left with the diocese. Sounds like you were trying to disappear."

"I guess it was something like that."

"So you *are* in hiding."

"When you watch someone get murdered right in front of you, you start to wonder about a lot of things. So I guess you could say I'm in hiding. Maybe from myself."

"That kind of puts you in the same category as the fellow who lived in this apartment," Tindal said, gesturing at the room with a quick wave of his hand.

"I don't understand."

"The way he lived, it looks like he was hiding from something, too."

• • •

Tindal's questions resurrected the demons I had struggled for so long to put to rest. I had tried to forget the horrible murder I witnessed, but it always came back at me—and I replayed it over and over again in my mind.

The day it happened was very much like any other day in the life of a parish priest. I had just finished the morning Mass and had returned to the rectory, when a very distraught, dark-haired, young woman rushed through the front door and into my office at the other end of the foyer.

"Father," she said in a tone of voice that barely concealed her emotions, "I need your help!"

"What is it?" I asked as I gestured for her to sit down in a chair on the other side of my desk.

"My name is Miranda," she explained. "I'm not a member of this parish. I don't go to church very often." She paused to collect her thoughts, and then continued. "I was still hoping you might be able to help me."

"What is it you need?" I asked.

"It's my husband," she said tearfully. She pulled a tissue out of her purse and wiped it across her eyes. "He's getting more and more irrational. He thinks I'm seeing someone else."

"Are you seeing someone else?" I asked gently.

"No. I have never been unfaithful to him. I have never given him any reason to doubt me. Yet, he is becoming more persistent in his accusations. Last night . . ." She paused again, pulled another tissue out of her purse, and wiped the tears from her eyes. "Last night," she continued, "he became very violent. He threatened to kill me if he found out I was seeing another man."

"*Your husband sounds like he's delusional,*" I said. "*Did he do anything more than threaten you?*"

"*No. He looked like he was going to hit me, but then he backed away. He seemed completely lost. He didn't seem to know where he was, or what he was doing. Then he walked outside. When he returned a few minutes later, he was his old self again.*"

"*It sounds like your husband is having a mental breakdown,*" I speculated. "*Do you have any children?*"

"*No. Just me.*"

"*Do you have any relatives who live nearby?*"

"*Just my mother,*" she said, reaching into her purse for another tissue.

"*You need to stay with her,*" I said firmly. "*Your husband needs professional help. If you talk to him at all, you need to do it over the telephone, not in person. His obsessions could cause him to do something terrible. Something you would both regret.*"

"*I don't know what to do . . .*"

Suddenly, the front door of the rectory burst violently open and smashed against the wall. A tall, bearded man with fierce, angry eyes rushed into the rectory. He was holding a pistol. When he saw Miranda and me sitting in my office, he strode quickly across the foyer.

He paused for a moment in front of her. For a few precious seconds, I was frozen, unable to act.

"*No, Waldo!*" Miranda screamed. "*Don't do . . .*"

As she held one hand up in the air to protect herself, her husband fired a single shot into her head. She slumped to the floor and disappeared on the other side of the desk, while I remained seated.

Her husband stared at the pistol. He seemed not to comprehend what he had just done. When he looked at me, his eyes were vacant, puzzled. He seemed to be fixated on my collar, which I had neglected to take off after the morning Mass. When he raised his head slightly and stared directly into my eyes, I was certain he was going to shoot me next. It was a look I had never seen before. It seemed to come from some lost world the deranged and delusional husband alone inhabited. A place where sane thoughts get lost in the darkness and are transformed into madness and obsessive fears of malignant, overpowering threats and betrayals.

He looked down at the lifeless body of his wife, crumpled up on the floor. Then he looked at me again with the same puzzled, uncomprehending expression. Someone must have seen him rush into *the rectory, gun drawn, because we suddenly heard the sound of a police siren in the distance. He stared at me, and then he turned and rushed out of the rectory.*

I answered endless questions from the police and detectives who strode into the rectory moments later. As they led me out of my office, I glanced down at the lifeless body of the woman. One of her arms was stretched across the floor, her palm open and blood smeared. A small hole in her hand indicated that the bullet had passed through her palm before entering her head. Her other hand was still thrust deeply into her purse, as though she was trying to extract another tissue to wipe her eyes.

The blood-smeared, open palm with the bullet hole was seared into my memory. That was a picture I could never erase from my mind, not even after I took a leave of absence from the priesthood and moved out of the rectory and into my apartment near Downtown San Diego. That was the picture that would keep me awake at night, often listening to my radiator belching and moaning on the other side of the room as I stared into the darkness, unable to sleep.

They never found the woman's husband. He disappeared, as though swallowed up by some abyss. Perhaps it was the abyss he carried inside of himself—the one I saw in his eyes moments after he shot his wife in the head. I continued to remember that look months later when I was stumbling around inside my own abyss, searching for a way out of the darkness. The police questioned me further about what had happened that day, but I was of little help to them. Like the woman's husband, I too wanted only to disappear and be left alone with my thoughts.

Why did his wife come to see me that morning? Why not someone else, since she was not a member of my parish? Why did her husband show up moments later? Was he following her? Or was it pure coincidence? Was he driving past the rectory, saw his wife's car parked outside, and his obsessions and suspicions raged out of control? Had his own religious background made it impossible for him to shoot a priest? Did the mere fact that I had forgotten to take off my collar after the Mass save my life?

My obsessive nature would not allow my subconscious mind to put the incident to rest. It preyed on me, often attacking my emotional vulnerabilities during both my waking and sleeping hours. It was relentless, and sometimes so debilitating I would not leave my apartment for days. Instead, I would sit with the window shades closed, staring at the few glimmers of light that fell across the smoke-stained walls. As I stared at those walls, I imagined all the other lost souls who had sat in the same chair, slept in the same bed with the deep indentations in the mattress, contemplating the same tricks of fate that had led them to this dark, depressing studio apartment.

Mostly, I was filled with guilt. I had not acted. I was frozen with fear. There was time enough for me to get up from my desk and put my body between the distraught woman and her enraged husband. Perhaps my collar would have protected her, as it apparently did me. Instead, I sat on the other side of the desk, watching the horrible event occur, not being able to act because I was terrified my own life was about to come to an abrupt end.

My mission as a priest was to serve others, but I had failed. I had not acted to save a human life. I was too worried about my own safety. I had to live with that awful truth.

CHAPTER TWO

Most mornings I jogged over to Balboa Park. On some mornings, I jogged north for a few blocks and then continued straight west on Beech Street until it dead ended near the San Diego Harbor. Later, I would return to my apartment via one of the streets north or south of Beech Street.

I enjoyed the alternate route because I could see the blue waters of the harbor almost from the moment I turned west. That route had another advantage: it enabled me to jog past the St. Joseph's Catholic Church.

St. Joseph's was not my parish, but I had visited it many times before I took my leave of absence. When I jogged past it, I always stopped for a few seconds and stared at the three huge wooden doors at the top of the concrete steps. I often thought about going inside, but I never did.

This time it was different. With Tindal's comments regarding the murder I had witnessed still fresh in my mind, I decided to go inside the church. I was not seeking some earthshaking revelations into my inner demons. I just wondered what it would feel like to be back in a church.

Inside the vestibule, a custodian was mopping the tile floor. Boxes of clothing and food items were stacked below a "Donations" sign taped to one of the walls. I slipped quietly past the custodian, walked into the church, and sat down in one of the pews next to a concrete pillar.

The early morning sunlight entered the windows high on the southern wall and streaked across the pews near the front of the church. The white, marble statue of the crucified Christ hovered high on the wall behind the altar. Confessionals were located in the shadows along both the northern and southern walls. I impulsively decided to sit inside one of the confessionals while I collected my thoughts. I looked behind me to make certain the custodian was not watching. Then I walked over to a confessional and stepped inside. As the door creaked shut, I sat in the darkness and thought of the many times I had listened to parishioners confess their sins while I sat on the other side of a confessional.

How does a priest confess his sins to himself? My theology classes never covered that possibility. Nor could I remember if there was a sin of cowardice?

That opened a Pandora's box of raw emotions and unresolved anxieties. I felt immediately uncomfortable and out of place in the confessional. I realized I did not belong on either side of the thin, wooden panel that separated the priests from the parishioners.

That wooden panel is nothing compared to the insurmountable walls that separate me from the rest of the human race. I want only to hide behind those walls, barricaded inside my private confessional where the word COWARD echoes like a constantly ringing church bell in the darkness. I have my own sins to deal with. I have no time for the sins of others.

I quickly stepped out of the confessional and strode out of the church.

• • •

When I returned to my apartment, I stopped in the foyer to check my mail. It was the usual assortment of junk mail. I don't know that I should have expected anything different. I had never given my new address to anyone. As I looked up from my mail, I noticed a note pinned to a bulletin board on the wall next to a fire alarm. It read, "Apartment 312 needs driver to help wheelchair resident. Will pay $10 an hour. If interested, take this note and meet me here at 8 a.m. tomorrow, March 23rd."

I unpinned the note, placed it in my shirt pocket, and walked down the hallway toward my apartment. At the end of the hallway, Detective Tindal was staring out the window, his back turned toward me.

"Back again?" I asked.

"Just made one last sweep of your neighbor's apartment," he said, turning and nodding.

"Find anything interesting?"

"Nope. Like I said before, there's no sign that he ever really lived there."

"Maybe you were right when you said he was probably setting it up to peddle drugs."

I started to insert the key into my apartment door.

"Wait a minute," he said suddenly. "I have a few more questions I need to ask you."

"Okay."

"Where were you last night?"

"Home. Why?"

"There was another incident in the park."

"What happened this time?"

"A park employee found the body of the homeless man who heard the gunshot the night your neighbor was killed."

"Another murder?"

"Could be a murder, or it could be he died from natural causes. We'll know more after the autopsy."

"So what is it you want from me?"

"Some of the detectives who were examining the crime scene where your neighbor was killed saw you in the park the other day. They thought you stopped and talked to the homeless man who died there last night."

"I saw a homeless man sitting near one of the fig trees," I replied defensively. "But, no, I didn't talk to him."

"Did . . ."

"Why do you keep assuming that somehow I'm involved in this? I jog over to the park almost every morning. It's how I start my day."

"People around you seem to die rather unexpectedly."

"I can't help it that a mentally unbalanced man kills his wife in front of me," I said. I struggled to control the overpowering sense of guilt I felt every time I was reminded of my failure to protect the woman who had come to me looking for help. "Or that a drug dealer moves into the apartment across the hallway from me. Or that a homeless man dies in Balboa Park."

"No, you can't help that," Tindal agreed. "But there may be another one, too."

"Another *what*?"

"The old man who died in his bathtub didn't have a heart attack as the coroner first suspected. He drowned. The coroner can't figure out how an otherwise healthy man drowned in six inches of water."

• • •

Something woke me up that night. I don't know what it was. It could have been a noise, a presence, or maybe some deeply felt instinct that told me I was not alone. I looked down at the thin sliver of hallway light that filtered under the door of my apartment and settled on the carpet. I watched as a shadow slipped slowly across the light. I heard the doorknob turn ever so gently. There was a long pause, and then the shadow slipped slowly out of the light and disappeared.

I was unable to fall asleep again until early morning. My thoughts kept alternating between the fact that I was obviously a suspect in a string of unexplained deaths in the area, and the noises I thought I kept hearing in the hallway.

How could I possibly be a murder suspect?

That possibility was so unfathomable I could not process it through any normal pattern of thinking about myself. In a few short months, I had gone from being a simple parish priest living a fairly mundane life, to apparently being at the top of a list of homicide suspects. I wanted only to retreat from the human race, and yet I seemed to have accumulated a lot of people who were either intentionally or unintentionally intruding into my life.

• • •

I had no real desire to take on a part-time job, but I was desperately in need of money to supplement the small check the diocese deposited in my meager checking account every month. Driving a van for a wheelchair-bound resident of my apartment seemed about as non-intrusive to my lifestyle as anything I had seen in the help-wanted section of the local newspaper. Since I still had my driver's license, I decided to see if it was something I could tolerate; or whether it would send me back to my apartment to read my books on philosophy and theology, while I absentmindedly rearranged the individual squares on my Rubik's Cube.

After breakfast, I locked my apartment door and walked out to the front foyer. An older, distinguished-looking man with distinctive, dark-brown eyes, a slightly pointed chin, and neat, closely trimmed, gray beard was sitting next to the mailboxes in a motorized wheelchair. He was dressed in what appeared to be an expensive business suit, and he had a leather briefcase on his lap. The rest of his attire did not fit the business image he was apparently trying to create. He wore a captain's cap, red bowtie, and both of his feet and ankles were bandaged and resting on the wheelchair's footrests. The wheelchair had a reddish-burgundy leather seat and backrest with matching leather pouches strapped to the armrests.

It had some deep scrapes and scratches on the frame, suggesting that it was an older model that had been handled rather roughly over the years.

"You are late," he said without looking in my direction.

"How did you know it was . . ."

"You have my note," he said, gesturing at the piece of paper I was holding in my hand. "I have much to do today. We can introduce ourselves in my van. As you can see, I am not able to drive myself to my business appointments."

He pressed a switch on the wheelchair, and I held the door open for him. He instructed me on how to help him get into the middle seat of the white van and store the wheelchair in the trunk. After we were settled into the van, he instructed me to drive toward the Downtown area. He said nothing more for a very long time. Finally, I decided to break the silence.

"My name is Justin Moore," I said.

"I know your name," he replied quickly.

"How . . ."

"It's my business to know things like that. I'm an accountant. You can call me A. C. I work for an international firm with worldwide affiliates. We are researching some new business opportunities in this area. I'm conducting a feasibility study. I will be paying you in cash to act as my driver. That's all you need to know about me."

He said nothing more, except to direct me through a maze of city streets until we entered an industrial section filled with weathered warehouses and other older buildings.

"Turn left here and park next to that warehouse," he said suddenly.

I pulled up to an old, wooden warehouse that was surrounded by other buildings with graffiti splashed across the brick and wooden walls. I walked around to the back of the van, pulled out the wheelchair, and helped him get into it.

"You wait here," he said.

He pressed the switch on the armrest, and the wheelchair moved slowly across the concrete parking lot to the front door of the warehouse. A partially concealed figure pushed the door open, and A. C. disappeared inside the building as the door slowly closed behind him. I leaned back in the van and waited.

On the other side of the street, some apparently homeless men were sitting on the front steps of an abandoned home with boarded-up windows and doors. They took turns sipping on a bottle of wine. Rap music poured out of another boarded-up home. Several heavily tattooed men suddenly drifted out of that building, climbed into two cars and a pick-up truck, and drove away.

I looked in the direction of the door where A. C. had entered the warehouse. Then I looked at the glove compartment. I glanced again at the warehouse door and reached over to open the glove compartment, which was empty except for the automobile registration. The owner of the van was listed as "EWE International."

I suddenly heard the warehouse door open. I quickly thrust the registration form back into the glove compartment and slammed the door shut. I immediately stepped out of the van and helped A. C. get into the middle seat. Once again, he directed me through a maze of city streets.

After another long silence, he finally asked, "Where do you have the greatest concentration of homeless people in this city?"

"Probably on the eastern end of the Downtown area."

"Take me there."

"May I ask what kind of business you're in?" I said as I glanced into the rearview mirror.

"You may ask. But we will need to have that conversation some other time," he replied tersely.

As we drove further east, many abandoned homes and boarded-up commercial buildings were visible on both sides of the street. There were several groups of homeless men gathered in front of a building with the words, "East Side Rescue Mission," painted across one wall. Some of the men were standing next to shopping carts piled high with plastic bottles and other items they had apparently pulled out of nearby dumpsters.

"Stop here!" A. C. said suddenly.

"Here?" I asked.

"Yes. Let me out."

I quickly pulled over to the curb and helped him get out of the van and into his wheelchair.

"Meet me back here in two hours," he said.

"Are you sure you don't want me to go with you?" I asked.

"No."

"This looks like a pretty rough neighborhood."

"Not as rough as many I've seen," he said as he pressed the switch on the armrest of his wheelchair. "You may take the van anywhere you like. But meet me back here in two hours."

I watched as the wheelchair moved down the street and disappeared into a large group of homeless men and women standing on the sidewalk.

• • •

What have I stumbled into?

That question surged through my mind as soon as I drove away. I was beginning to feel more than a little uneasy about my part-time job. I was already a suspect in the police investigations into several unusual deaths and homicides, and now I had a new employer who refused to give me his name. Instead, he insisted that I call him a shortened form of the word accountant—A. C. Then he asked me to wait for him outside a warehouse in an area that looked like it could be used as a setting for a film about a drug cartel.

What kind of business is he in that he needs to know where he can find the largest concentration of homeless people in San Diego? Can I afford to be associated with someone like this?

As I drove away, I decided to take a closer look at EWE International, the company that owned the van I was driving. If I was going to be a driver for the wheelchair-bound, elderly man who called himself A. C., I needed to know if he worked for a legitimate company. Two hours gave me plenty of time to drive over to the Downtown city library and do a quick Internet search for EWE International. I needed the money badly, but I didn't know if I needed it so badly that I was willing to be connected to someone who appeared to be involved in something that might very well be illegal—and even dangerous.

The San Diego City Library had opened only three months earlier, and I had never been inside. From a distance, I could see the multi-storied, glass, and reinforced-concrete and steel-frame structure rise into the sky. With its huge domed top, it looked more like a space observatory than a big-city library.

A car pulled out of a metered parking space about two blocks from the library, and I pulled in right behind it. I stuffed four more quarters into the slot on the side of the parking meter and quickly walked over to the library. When I stepped into the first floor, I paused to look up at the huge ceiling. Whoever had designed the library had created a futuristic look to compliment the exterior of the building. The large glass windows, spaced several stories high around the outer walls, allowed the blue sky and several other

Downtown skyscrapers to be visible from almost every angle on the first floor. It also created the surreal effect that the building was lifting off into space.

I asked a librarian where I might find the computer room, and she directed me to the fourth floor. I took the escalator up to the second floor, and the elevator to the fourth floor. There were two empty chairs next to the tables reserved for public Internet use. I sat down behind one of the computers and took a deep breath. I said a quick silent prayer for some guidance in determining whether or not I could afford to keep my part-time job when I was already viewed with such suspicion by the San Diego Police. I typed in the words EWE International and waited. Moments later, the words, "No listing for EWE International available" appeared on the screen. I leaned back in my chair and stared out the window at the corporate-owned skyscrapers on the other side of the street.

Just what kind of business is he in that it doesn't even show up on an Internet search?

• • •

A. C. was waiting for me when I pulled up to the curb in front of the East Side Rescue Mission. I helped him into the van, and we drove away. I glanced occasionally at my rearview mirror to see what he was doing in the seat behind me. He appeared to be sorting through some papers he had pulled out of his briefcase. Finally, I decided to break the silence.

"Did you find what you were looking for?" I asked.

In the rearview mirror, I saw him look up at me briefly. His gaze immediately shifted back to the papers that were sprawled across his lap.

"I saw the same look in their eyes that I have seen so many times before," he replied evasively.

"Whose eyes?" I asked.

"There are too many of them," he said, ignoring me. "Far too many. Something needs to be done to change all of this. But no one seems to have the courage to do what needs to be done."

"And what is that?" I asked.

"There are too many of them," he repeated.

He did not speak for the rest of the trip back to our apartment building. After I helped him out of the van and into his wheelchair, he said, "I won't need you tomorrow. I have some preliminary work to do on my report. Meet me by the mailboxes in two days. Same time. You may keep the keys to the van and use it if you need to run some errands."

He pressed a wad of cash into my hand and left in the wheelchair. I stared at the bills, wondering how my employer had earned the money—or if it had been stolen. As I closed the back door and prepared to lock the van, I noticed something lying on the floormat near where he had been sitting. It was a pencil drawing of some homeless men and women he had apparently met on the streets near the East Side Rescue Mission. They were posed in a group, as though he had asked them to stand together so he could draw them.

I glanced quickly at A. C.'s wheelchair as it disappeared into the front door of our apartment building. Then I studied the details in the pencil drawing. It was not just some quick sketch. It was an impressive, beautifully detailed drawing. The details were so realistic that the men and women looked like they were alive inside the drawing. The shadings and shadows A. C. had created by deftly smearing the pencil marks in various subtle ways reminded me of something I had seen before, but I could not remember where. It looked much more like a work of art than a pencil drawing.

I folded the drawing, placed it in my pocket, and walked over to the front door of my apartment building. I quickly checked my mailbox and walked down the hallway. As I inserted the key into my apartment door, I heard footsteps behind me. Turning, I saw a young woman with dark-black hair standing in the doorway of the apartment where the two former occupants had died so suddenly and unexpectedly. She was an attractive, slightly foreign-looking woman in her midtwenties.

"Good morning," she said, smiling as she stepped into the hallway.

"Good morning," I replied awkwardly.

"I just moved in," she said warmly. "My name is Ilsa."

"Justin," I replied nervously. "I live . . . well, you can see I live right across the hallway from you."

She seemed to sense that I was nervous and uneasy.

"Are you okay with having me as your new neighbor," she said teasingly.

"Yes . . . I . . . It's just that there aren't too many women living in this building."

"I work nearby. It's convenient," she replied, glancing at her watch. "I have to be going. Nice to meet you."

• • •

The next morning, I tried to reestablish some of the daily rituals
I had practiced as a parish priest. I thought that perhaps they
would give me a sense of security that I no longer felt in my new
life. I struggled to pray for spiritual guidance, but my efforts were
of little avail. I tried saying a rosary, but that also failed as my
thoughts kept wandering into areas more directly related to the
circumstances of my life after I had taken a leave of absence from
the priesthood.

Finally, I gave up and decided instead to jog down Sixth Avenue.
I was about to jog across the Laurel Street Bridge, when a police car
with two officers pulled up to the curb next to me. The heavy-set
officer in the passenger seat rolled down the window and gestured
for me to come over.

"Detective Tindal wants you to come Downtown with us," he said.

"Why?"

"Just get in," he said, nodding at the back door.

I opened the car door, slipped into the seat, and we drove toward
the Downtown area. Minutes later, we entered a parking structure
underneath the San Diego Police Headquarters. We took an elevator up to the third floor, and the officers ushered me into a small
interrogation room. I sat down on one side of a wooden table. Tindal
walked in moments later and sat down in a chair on the other side.
The other officers quickly left the room.

"I suppose you're wondering why I asked you to come down
here?" he said.

"I figure it has something to do with that homeless man who
died in the park. The one you figured had been murdered."

"No, he died from natural causes."

"So what is it then?" I asked. "Why'd you ask me to come here?"

"We've been keeping an eye on you. And the company you keep.
We know you've been driving an older man in a wheelchair around
in a white van. What can you tell me about him?"

"Nothing."

"Nothing?"

"He has told me nothing. Not even his real name. He says he's
an accountant. He told me to abbreviate that to A. C. That's all I
know about him."

"Is he paying you?"

"Of course he's paying me. I pick up odd jobs wherever I can. I need to pay my bills. Certainly that's no crime."

Tindal ignored my response. He lit a cigarette, puffed deeply on it, and rubbed his other hand across his cheek.

"How did you meet him?" he asked.

"He left a note on the bulletin board next to our mailboxes. It said he needed a driver. Why is he so important to you?"

Tindal suddenly stood up, walked over to one of the windows overlooking the city streets, and puffed on the cigarette. "We have reason," he said, "to believe he might be working with one of the drug cartels that is trying to move into this area."

"Why do you think that?"

"We have sources."

"So what do you want from me?"

"We also think he might be involved in the murders of the people who lived in the apartment across the hall from you."

"You say *murders*. Are you now convinced that both of them were murdered?"

"One of them for sure. It's a pretty good bet the other one didn't die from natural causes."

"So what do you want from me?" I repeated.

"We want you to keep an eye on him. Report anything to us that you think is unusual, especially anything that might reveal who he's working for."

"The registration form for the van lists EWE International as the owner," I said.

"I know, but it doesn't exist," Tindal replied as he turned and looked back at me. "It appears to be a completely fictitious company."

"I don't know what to make of him, but I don't think you have him pegged right. He doesn't seem like the type—"

"Maybe this will help change your mind," Tindal said as he walked back to where I was sitting and pushed a photograph of a blood-splattered body across the table.

"Who is this?" I asked as I studied the photograph.

"Your former neighbor."

"The one who was killed in Balboa Park?"

"Same one."

"What does this have to do with A. C. and EWE International?"

"I have no idea who A. C. is, or what his real name might be," Tindal said, angrily jabbing his finger at the photograph. "I only know that a woman who lives in an apartment near the Laurel Street Bridge heard a gunshot the night your former neighbor was killed. She looked out her third-story window and saw a light-colored van race out of Balboa Park and disappear down Sixth Avenue."

"There are a lot of light-colored vans in San Diego," I insisted. "How do you know it's this one?"

"We don't. But since this person you call A. C. and your next-door neighbor who was killed lived in the same apartment building, and a light-colored van was seen leaving the murder scene, and your new employer drives a white van and works for a company that doesn't seem to exist—well, that adds up to a lot of suspicious coincidences in my book."

"A. C. can't drive," I said. "He was in some kind of accident."

"Then he probably had another driver before you," Tindal replied as he puffed deeply on the cigarette and looked back in the direction of the window overlooking the city streets.

· · ·

That night I sat in the darkness and listened to the clicking sound of my Rubik's Cube as I turned and twisted it in every possible direction. The curtains and shades were drawn, and only a few streaks of moonlight filtered into the studio apartment.

I had purchased the Rubik's Cube at a Salvation Army store a few months earlier, but I had never solved the puzzle. Still, I enjoyed twisting and turning it in the hope that maybe someday I would find a solution to the elaborate puzzle some eccentric genius had concocted to baffle the less gifted. Some nights I just kept playing with it in the darkness in the hope that maybe when I turned the lights back on in the morning, the Rubik's Cube would have miraculously solved itself.

It never happened.

Still, it gave me a chance to do something with my hands while I sat in the darkness, alone with my thoughts, pondering the many might-have-beens in my life. Often, while I listened to the clicking sound of the Rubik's Cube, the same questions came back to me.

How did I get here? How did I go from being a parish priest with a rather boring life to a recluse who sits in the darkness of a studio apartment trying to solve a Rubik's Cube I cannot even see?

Often, as I sat in the darkness, I replayed in my mind the incident that was most responsible for the bizarre direction my life had taken. Usually, I reinvented the way it might have ended in the hope that maybe once I turned on the lights, the Rubik's Cube would have solved itself, and I would have emerged from the rectory that fateful day with my faith in myself intact. I had vivid memories of the moments shortly before and after her husband burst into the rectory.

"It sounds like your husband is having a mental breakdown," I speculated. "Do you have any children?"

"No. Just me."

"Do you have any relatives who live nearby?"

"Just my mother," she said, reaching into her purse for another tissue.

"You need to stay with her," I said firmly. "Your husband needs professional help. If you talk to him at all, you need to do it over the telephone, not in person. His obsessions could cause him to do something terrible. Something you would both regret."

"I don't know what to do. . . ."

Suddenly, the front door of the rectory burst violently open and smashed against the wall. A thin, bearded man with fierce, angry eyes rushed into the rectory. He was holding a pistol. When he saw his wife and me sitting in my office, he strode quickly across the foyer.

He paused for a moment in front of her. For a few precious seconds, I was frozen, unable to act.

"No, Waldo!" Miranda screamed. "Don't do . . ."

I knew I had to act quickly. Otherwise, I would be a witness to a horrible murder. I stepped out from behind my desk and positioned myself between the woman and her angry husband.

His eyes were vacant, puzzled. He seemed to be fixated on my collar, which I had neglected to take off after the morning mass. When he raised his head slightly and stared directly into my eyes, I was certain he was going to shoot me and then his wife.

Instead, he lowered the gun. He looked at me again with the same puzzled, uncomprehending expression. Someone must have seen him rush into the rectory, gun drawn, because we heard the sound of a police siren in the distance. He stared at me again, and then he turned and rushed out of the rectory.

That was the way I reimagined what might have happened if I had not cowered in fear behind my desk while he fired a bullet into his wife's head. Instead, every day as I jogged over to Balboa Park or the harbor, I tried to erase from my memory the nightmarish image of the woman's blood-smeared open palm with the bullet hole.

I could not deny that I was having a deep crisis of faith.

Why? Lord, Heavenly Father, why her? Why me?

I twisted the Rubik's Cube one last time in the darkness. Then I turned on the light next to my reading chair and looked down at what I had done to the Rubik's Cube. It was a mishmash of different colors on all four sides.

It had not solved itself.

• • •

I was drinking a cup of coffee and reading the newspaper near the big fountain in Balboa Park when I heard footsteps behind me. Turning, I saw the young, foreign-looking woman who had identified herself as my new neighbor approaching. Ilsa was dressed in tan work pants and shirt, and she was carrying a canvas backpack with shoulder straps.

"Mind if I join you?" she asked.

"Yes, of course," I said, removing the newspaper that cluttered the small table and gesturing for her to sit down.

"Do you have today off?" she asked as she set the backpack on the table.

"Unless I'm driving a van for an elderly wheelchair-bound man, I have every day off," I replied. "And you?"

"I'm working today."

"In Balboa Park?"

"I'm an entomologist."

"A *what?*"

"I study bugs," she said, laughing.

"What kind of bugs?"

"Just about all of them. Right now, I'm doing some contract work for the supervisors of this park." She pointed at some withered flowers on a nearby bush. "They want to know why many of the plants are not blossoming this spring."

"I read about that in the paper."

"It's the bees. Something has been killing them, and they want me to try to find out why." She reached into her canvas bag and pulled out a clear, plastic container. She removed the lid and pointed at several dead bees curled up at the bottom. "It's these little guys here. I just collected them this morning."

"The article I read said it was probably 'parasitic flies.'"

"That's one possibility," she said, placing the lid on the container and returning it to the backpack.

"Didn't Einstein say something about the disappearance of the honeybees, and what it would mean to the human race?" I asked.

"He supposedly said, 'If the bee disappears from the surface of the earth, man would have no more than four years to live.' We don't know if he really said it, or if someone attributed it to him."

"What do other scientists think?"

"They would agree with Einstein, even if he didn't say it."

I paused to study her eyes more closely. I didn't know if I should tell her what had happened in her apartment before she moved in. I finally decided I had no choice.

"Look," I said, "when we first met in the hallway, I was a little nervous. . . ."

"I noticed."

"I didn't know if anyone told you that the last two people who rented your apartment died rather mysteriously. One died in the apartment, and the other was murdered in Balboa Park."

"The manager told me."

"And you still rented the apartment?"

"Yes," she replied with little emotion.

"Aren't you a little concerned?" I asked, surprised by her casual response to my question.

"Not as concerned as I am about something else."

"What's that?"

"The bees that are dying in this park."

• • •

There was a bar a few blocks from where I lived that was called Jake's Club. I wasn't what you would call "a regular," but I would occasionally stop there and sip on a glass of wine while I watched the television set attached to the wall in a far corner of the room. I had no idea who Jake was, or if he still owned the bar or had been dead for a long time. I had heard some of the customers call the bartender "Sid," and that was as much as I knew about Jake's Club.

The night before I was to meet A. C. again, there was no one else in Jake's Club except Sid and me. He was washing glasses and occasionally glancing at the television set, while I sipped on my glass of wine and pondered whether or not I should continue driving a van for the mysterious elderly gentleman who worked for a fictitious business named EWE International.

Suddenly, a television reporter closed the evening news with a brief update about my former neighbor, the one who had been murdered in Balboa Park. The reporter said, "Police have still not positively identified the victim, although they found a photograph of him in his wallet. The wallet apparently contained no other identification." The reporter concluded the coverage of the story by requesting that "anyone who might know the victim is asked to contact the San Diego Police Department."

As the photograph of the Balboa Park victim came on the television screen, Sid looked up from the glasses he was washing. "He was in here a few days before they found him in the park," he said.

"The one up there on the television screen?" I asked.

"Yup. Same one. Sat right where you're sitting. I'll never forget him. I've had a lot of strange characters come in here over the years, but he was the strangest."

"In what way?"

"I can't describe it. It was . . . his eyes. There just didn't seem to be anyone behind them."

"Think he was on drugs?"

"No, it was something else. I've seen just about every kind of drug addict in my life. Used to work in one of the seedier bars farther south. This one . . . This fellow seemed like only a part of him was here, and the rest of him was someplace else. Some place farther away than I've ever been."

I looked back at the television as the photograph of the murder victim disappeared from the screen and was replaced by a commercial for a new kind of shampoo.

"Did he talk about himself at all?" I asked.

"Not a word. Didn't even order a drink. He just sat on that stool, looking like he was trying to figure out where he was and what he was doing here. Then he just suddenly up and left."

"Did you report any of this to the police?"

"Ya, I did. Right after I saw that photograph of him on the television for the first time."

"What'd they say?"

"Nothing. They just wanted to know if he was with anyone else, or if he left alone."

"*Did* he leave with someone else?"

"Nope. I heard a horn honk outside in the parking lot. Shortly after that, he just up and left. I don't know if that had anything to do with him leaving. Television has been saying police think it was a drug deal gone bad, but I don't know. Seems to me that he was just one of those people who forget who they are."

"An amnesiac?"

"Ya, one of those."

CHAPTER THREE

I **was apprehensive about** what I was learning, but I decided to keep my part-time job as A. C.'s driver. Maybe it was the money. Maybe it was curiosity about my wheelchair-bound employer. Maybe it was some sense I had that it was taking me someplace in my life that I had never been before, wherever that might be. Or maybe it was because I didn't really care where I was going.

The most compelling reason was something quite unrelated to all of the other reasons. I began to wonder if perhaps I'd been given an opportunity to make amends for what I had failed to do in the church rectory. Maybe I'd been positioned to stop something even more terrible from happening, something A. C. and EWE International were planning.

Whatever the case, I met A. C. by the mailboxes the next morning, and we immediately went outside, got into the van, and drove away. A. C. sat quietly in the middle seat and did not seem to want to engage in conversation, except to direct me to the parts of San Diego where he had meetings.

Everyone he met that morning was dressed in similarly styled, dark business suits, and most of them carried briefcases. Each meeting took only a few minutes. There was no pattern to the places we visited. He asked me to remain in the van while he talked to two businessmen on top of a Downtown parking structure near the El Cortez Hotel. Then he directed me to drive about five miles north of the Downtown area to Presidio Park, where he met with another businessman who stepped out of a small adobe building to greet him. After that, we drove south back through the Downtown area, where he met with a businessman in a dark business suit underneath the San Diego side of the Coronado Bridge. Later, after crossing through the Downtown area again, he met with two women in similarly colored business suits on a sidewalk near Pacific Beach, while the ocean surf roared in the background. Yet another meeting was with a businessman who stepped out of the Downtown federal building as A. C.'s wheelchair approached the front door.

After that meeting, A. C. directed me to drive him over to Balboa Park. I parked the van in one of the parking lots behind the restaurants and shops. "You'll have to push me over to the San Diego Museum of Art," he said. "The battery is very low. I need to save what power is left."

As I pushed him across the street, I saw a huge banner on the wall above the front door of the museum advertising the "Renaissance Art Exhibition" that was currently the featured travelling exhibit on loan to the museum. We paid the entrance fee, and he directed me to one of the exhibit rooms in the rear of the first floor of the museum. Security guards in business suits were positioned all along the hallway.

"Wait here," A. C. said as we turned into one of the exhibit rooms. He directed his wheelchair into an adjacent exhibit room, and I remained behind within view of the heavily guarded, rare art exhibition.

While I waited for him to return, I surveyed the art works hanging on the walls. They were paintings and drawings by Da Vinci, Michelangelo, Raphael, and other Renaissance masters. I had remembered reading about the opening of this new exhibit in the newspaper, but I had forgotten about it. Even at a glance, these paintings by the Renaissance masters were stunningly realistic. The biblical and historical figures seemed almost to leap off the canvases.

My real interest, however, was in what A. C. was doing in the next room. As I pretended to study the Renaissance paintings, I edged closer to the large doorway separating the two exhibit rooms. I could hear A. C. and another man talking out of sight, just around the corner.

"So, where are we in all of this?" the man asked.

"It is not time yet," A. C. replied. "It would be premature."

"If not now, when?"

"When everything is in place. It all takes time."

"Time is not something we have a lot of."

"I know they are impatient."

"They may not wait much longer."

"Maybe I will have to go back and try to convince them it is in their best interests to wait."

"You may have to do that."

Suddenly, a group of tourists walked into the exhibit room where I was listening to A. C.'s conversation. They were following a tour guide who proceeded to escort them around the room while he described the history of each of the paintings hanging on the walls. Since his voice drowned out the conversation between A. C. and the man in the next room, I decided to join his group.

As the tour guide paused in front of a drawing behind a thick, glass display case, he explained, "This is an original early drawing by the great Italian artist, Michelangelo. It is called *St. Anna Metterza,* and it was inspired by Leonardo da Vinci's *Madonna with St. Anne.* As you can see, even with the barest rudiments of artistic equipment, in this case a simple pen and ink, Michelangelo's artistic genius still shines through."

I lingered behind and continued to study the pencil drawing long after the tour guide and his group had moved elsewhere in the room. As I studied the details in Michelangelo's pencil drawing, I flashed back to my days in the seminary and wished I had paid closer attention to church history during the Renaissance period. I also realized why A. C.'s drawing of the homeless people had seemed vaguely familiar. It had reminded me of some of the Renaissance sketches I remembered from my art history courses. It was also very much like the one Michelangelo had drawn.

• • •

Later, as we drove out of the park, A. C. was more talkative. "Did you enjoy the Renaissance paintings and sketches?" he asked.

"Yes, of course," I replied. "They're very impressive."

"I like to stare at those paintings until I feel like I'm inside of them, looking out," he said. "Have you ever done that?"

"No."

"You should. It makes you wonder how Da Vinci and Michelangelo and the other Renaissance geniuses would view us."

"I'm afraid they would find us rather shallow."

"Perhaps we *are* rather shallow," A. C. replied. "Perhaps we could use someone like them in the modern world. Art is the force that drives the universe. Did you know that?"

"I've never thought about it," I admitted.

"You should. Science is important, of course. But it could not exist without the power of art behind it. The imagination leads the way for all human progress."

"I think Einstein said something like that," I speculated.

"Yes, I know," A. C. replied.

I glanced out the window at a homeless man holding a "Will work for food" sign scribbled across a piece of cardboard. An elderly woman standing nearby held another sign with the message, "No more wars! The corruption is complete!"

"What do you make of all this?" A. C. asked.

"The signs?"

"No. Everything you have seen today."

"I don't understand."

"The people I met. Perhaps you are a little curious."

"I try not to think about things I don't understand," I replied evasively.

"Michelangelo and Da Vinci would be disappointed in you. Their artistic visions were inspired by the things they didn't understand."

"They were geniuses. I'm not."

"Perhaps you underestimate yourself. Perhaps there is more inside of you than you realize. . . . By the way, tomorrow I need you to drive me over to the International Business Forum at the Convention Center. After that, I will be gone for a time. We will discuss what I need you to do for me during my absence."

• • •

Maybe A. C. and EWE International are art traders—or art thieves!

That thought kept me awake long past my normal bedtime. It seemed to explain everything I had observed that day much better than the drug cartel theory Detective Tindal was pursuing.

Are they planning a heist of the Renaissance paintings in the museum of art?

The strange meetings with men and women in similarly styled business suits, the muffled conversation between A. C. and the unidentified man in the exhibit room next to the paintings by the Renaissance masters, A. C.'s sophisticated knowledge of art history, his pencil drawing—none of those things sounded like a criminal mastermind who was paving the way for a drug cartel to move into the San Diego region. They sounded more like someone who might be a very sophisticated art dealer—or art thief.

Once again, I thought about giving up my part-time job as his driver. And once again, I talked myself out of it. I convinced myself that I was in no danger. I was also more than a little intrigued by the way my path and A. C.'s path had intersected in our apartment building. I was simultaneously mystified and intrigued by whatever had brought us together. I felt some deep, subliminal need to find out why all of that had happened.

How did he even know I would be the one who would answer the note he had pinned to the bulletin board? Where did that come from?

My wheelchair-bound employer was no common criminal. Of that, I was certain. He was not like anyone I had ever met before. If he was a criminal, he was a very sophisticated and well-educated criminal. He gave the impression that he had traveled and experienced a great deal in his life. There was something about him that was simultaneously appealing, mystifying, and yet subtly threatening. I was convinced that he was a very powerful member of EWE International.

Yet, his power is in his mere presence more than anything tangible. Physically, he is fragile, even weak. Still, behind all of that apparent weakness and fragility, he exudes a quiet strength that seems to radiate outwards and pull people into his presence. How does all of that come together in one person?

In the middle of my ruminations, I must have nodded off. I don't know how long I was asleep when I was awakened by a voice in the hallway. I recognized it immediately as Ilsa's voice. She sounded very frightened, even panicked. When I opened the door, she rushed into my apartment.

"What's wrong?" I asked.

"I dreamt that there was someone in my apartment," she said. She glanced over her shoulder, looking back in the direction of her apartment door. "I heard voices. When I woke up, it all seemed so real."

"Do you want me to check it out for you?"

"No. There's no one there. I'm sure of it. It was just . . . very frightening. I was wondering if I could stay here with you tonight. Otherwise, I don't think I'll be able to get back to sleep."

"I only have one bed. No couch."

"I promise not to crowd you. You can put a row of pillows between us if that will make you more comfortable."

Without waiting for an answer, she crawled into bed and retreated to the far wall. I watched her for a few seconds as she closed her eyes and started breathing steadily. Then I set up a bed for myself on the floor. I decided I did not want her to wake up in the middle of the night and wonder who was sleeping next to her. I also felt uncomfortable with the idea of sharing a bed with someone I hardly knew.

I did not hear anything from her for the rest of the night. She seemed to be sleeping peacefully. Whatever had frightened her earlier did not seem to have a lasting effect.

When I awoke the next morning, she was gone, and there was a note on her pillow that read, "Thank you for letting me sleep in your bed. I hope I did not inconvenience you too much."

• • •

The next day, I followed behind A. C.'s wheelchair as we entered the first floor of the San Diego Convention Center. A huge banner at the entrance announced the gathering as the "International Business Forum." A crowd of businessmen and women milled around the booths and exhibits that filled the large, spacious arena. A food court with individual booths representing many of the world's fast food chains was located near the front entrance.

"Meet me back here in one hour," A. C. said as soon as we passed underneath the banner. "I need to meet with some of my associates."

As he drove away in his wheelchair, two men in business suits stepped out of adjacent booths and joined him. They walked on opposite sides of the wheelchair, looking very much like two security guards surveying the milling crowd of people for any threat to their client.

For a time I wandered among the exhibits, unsure of what to do during A. C.'s absence. As I passed one of the fast food booths, a middle-aged woman carrying an oversized purse stepped out of the crowd and started walking in my direction. As she came closer, I recognized her as Ruth Morgan, a woman who had done volunteer work for my parish. However, she looked much different than I remembered. Her clothing was worn and stained, and her arms and face were extremely tan, seemingly from overexposure to the sun. She reminded me of some of the homeless people I had seen gathered on the street the day A. C. had asked me to drop him off near the East Side Rescue Mission.

"Father Justin," she said, walking quickly over to where I was standing. "Do you remember me?"

"Yes, Ruth," I replied, "of course I remember you. How have you been?"

"Oh, I guess things could be better. But I'm doing okay. How about you?"

"I'm on leave. Probably forever. After what happened that day in the rectory, I just had to get away for a while."

"Yes. That was a terrible thing you had to witness," she replied sympathetically.

"Are you still working as a bank cashier?" I asked.

"Oh, no, I was terminated."

"Why?"

"An unfavorable job report. They said I was 'erratic,' whatever that means."

"You were the most organized and dependable volunteer we had in the diocese. What happened?"

"The insurance company wouldn't pay for my daughter's surgery, so I took out a loan on my house to pay for it. I didn't read the fine print. Lost everything. Then my daughter died. Everything just kind of fell apart after that. I guess I just stopped caring."

"I'm sorry. Where are you living now?"

"With some others who lost everything. We took over one of the foreclosed homes on Grape Street near Ivy Avenue. We're probably going to be evicted soon, but for now it's a roof over our heads. What about you? Where are you living?"

"In an apartment near the Downtown area."

"Are you working?" she asked.

"Odd jobs to pay the rent. That's the best I've been able to do."

"I saw you with a man in a wheelchair when you came in here."

"That's one of my odd jobs," I explained. "I'm his driver."

"It's better than not being able to find any work."

"I guess. So what brings you to this orgy of corporate power?"

"I have to make a brief presentation. If you hang around here, you'll see it in about forty-five minutes." She glanced at her wristwatch and added, "Look, I have to go. I need to get organized."

"Okay. Nice seeing you."

She smiled and turned to leave. Then she paused and looked back at me. "It was supposed to be you," she said.

"What?" I asked.

"I just couldn't do it," she said as she walked away.

• • •

I didn't know what to make of Ruth's parting words. She seemed to be struggling with her emotions during our chance encounter.

I assumed that whatever she was trying to communicate got tangled up in those emotions and came out sounding awkward and confusing.

While I waited for A. C. to return, I decided to explore some of the booths near the food court. As I wandered down the aisle separating two long rows of booths, I quickly came to the conclusion that the International Business Forum was a celebration of opulence and prosperity. It seemed that each of the booths was trying to outdo the other booths with extravagant, eye-catching displays. The more lavish displays featured strings of colorful balloons attached to the metal poles that supported the canvas roofs. Other booths had huge widescreen televisions that continuously advertised their company's many achievements in the world of international business.

Shortly after I started down the center aisle, I spotted an information kiosk off to my right. An attractive young woman in a gray business suit was standing behind a computer screen in the kiosk.

"Excuse me," I said, walking over to her. "Could you look up the location of one of the businesses that is attending this forum?"

"Of course," she replied. "What's the name?"

"EWE International."

"How do you spell it?" she asked.

"*E* as in eagle, *W* as in water, and *E* as in eagle . . . and then the word *International*."

"Let me see what we have on that business," she said, typing the information into the keyboard. She paused to study the screen and then shook her head. "Sorry, we have nothing on EWE International. Are you sure they're participating in this forum?"

"Well, no, I'm not certain. I just wanted to see if they might be here."

"Nope," she said, smiling and shaking her head again. "Doesn't look like it. Sorry."

I didn't know if EWE International would be participating in the International Business Forum. I thought perhaps it wouldn't, since it apparently didn't even exist as a legitimate business. It could be a secret subsidiary engaged in illegal criminal activities hidden within a respectable corporation. Still, I had decided to check anyway, on the outside chance that I might learn something—anything—about EWE International.

I still had some time to play with before I had to meet A. C. back at the food court, so I continued to walk down the aisle, exploring the business booths and displays. From what I could gather, there were companies from almost every country on the planet. It was obviously a very important and well-funded business forum.

As I was about to turn and walk back to the food court, I saw A. C.'s wheelchair off to my left. There was a small semicircle of businessmen and women, all of them dressed in dark-blue business suits, gathered around him. Some of them looked like the same people he had met the previous day at various locations throughout San Diego.

I tried to find a vantage point that would allow me to listen to their conversation, but there was nothing close enough to them to conceal my presence. Instead, I continued to watch from a distance. They seemed to be discussing something very seriously because their body language was very animated. Only A. C. seemed calm and restrained.

As I continued to try to get some kind of reading on what they were discussing, three of them stood and prepared to leave. The others started pushing papers into their briefcases, and A. C. stretched his arms and looked like he, too, was about to leave. I quickly turned and started walking back down the aisle.

As I walked toward the food court, I sensed a commotion off to my right. When I approached that area, I saw Ruth Morgan standing in an open space, holding a makeshift cardboard sign with the words "THE IBF IS A DEN OF THIEVES" scrawled across one side in bold, capital letters.

"They killed my daughter, and now they're killing me!" Ruth yelled in a loud, angry tone of voice. "They killed my daughter, and now they're killing me!"

As security guards converged on the area, she repeated the statement several times, almost like a ritualistic chant. Then she suddenly reached into her coat pocket, pulled out a revolver, and held the barrel against her temple.

"They killed my daughter, and now they're killing me!" she repeated as onlookers dove to the ground and the security guards instinctively stepped back.

Suddenly, the muzzle flashed and a loud, echoing explosion filled the area. Ruth slumped to the floor, blood pouring out of her temple. As others screamed in panic and dropped to the floor, I continued to stand there, staring at Ruth's lifeless body and blood-splattered sign.

• • •

A. C. and I drove in silence after we left the convention center. Finally, he spoke. "You knew that woman who killed herself, didn't you?" he asked.

"How did you know that?" I replied.

"I could tell."

"Yes, I knew her," I admitted.

"Do you know *why* she killed herself?"

"I talked to her briefly. She was down on her luck, lost her daughter. But she must have also been demonstrating against someone at the forum. She was holding a sign with the words 'The IBF is a Den of Thieves' scrawled across it."

"She may be right."

"About what?" I asked.

"The International Business Forum. They may be a den of thieves."

"Then why do you attend it?"

"Is it wrong for a thief to steal from a thief?" he asked.

"I don't understand."

"Nor should you. It seems like the world today glorifies and celebrates those who steal. Have you ever thought about that possibility?"

"Not really."

"It wasn't always that way," he explained. "Thieves were once dealt with rather severely. Amputations of their hands, drowning, even crucifixions—those were some of the punishments for thieves in earlier cultures."

"Someone at the forum must have been responsible for what happened to Ruth and her daughter," I speculated. "Otherwise, I don't see why she would have committed suicide while she held that protest sign."

"I'm very sorry about your friend," A. C. said with an emotionally distant, albeit kindly tone of voice. "No one should have to go through what she went through."

"No, they shouldn't," I agreed.

As we drove out of the Downtown area, he suddenly said, "Please take me over to the Mission Beach Pier."

"The pier?" I said.

"Yes, I'm meeting with some people over there tonight."

I drove north on Interstate 5, got off at Sea World Drive, and made my way over to Mission Beach on a series of narrow side roads. I found a parking place about a block from the pier and helped A. C. out of the van and into his wheelchair. As we approached the entrance to the pier, we passed a small registration room to our left with the sign "Hotel Office" attached to the outer wall next to the door.

The pier itself stretched well out into the ocean, and some blue and white tourist cottages were spaced along both of the outer railings almost to the middle of the pier. There were twenty numbered cottages with an additional six cottages with letters from A to F. Lights at the end of long poles were attached to the guardrail on the southern side of the pier. The end of the pier opened up onto a deck where some tourists were looking out over the ocean. Three fishermen next to them were dangling lines into the ocean waters far below the pier.

"This is the longest concrete pier on the West Coast," A. C. said. "Did you know that?"

"No, I didn't," I said.

"When you reach the end of it, it feels like you're entering another world. . . . This is as far as you need to go."

"You're going out there alone?" I asked.

"I'm meeting some business associates from out of town. They wanted to get a view of the beachfront properties. They said the end of this pier is the best place to get that view . . . I'll be with them for a few days while we discuss where we're at with my own project. So you can have the van for your personal use again. I'll put a note on the bulletin board by the mailboxes when I return and need you."

Before leaving, he paid me in cash and added an extra hundred dollars for gas money. He immediately pushed the switch on the armrest, and the wheelchair moved slowly to the end of the pier. I paused for a moment to listen to the waves smashing against the concrete pilings just below my feet. Then I walked back to the street, where I spotted a small bar that looked like it had a view of the ocean. I walked inside, ordered a glass of wine, and sat down next to a window overlooking the beach. I couldn't see the pier, but I could see some surfers riding shallow waves as the sun started to dip into the Pacific Ocean.

I sat by that window for some time, thinking about what had happened at the convention center only a few hours earlier. I didn't know what to make of it, except that another person had died in my presence, albeit this one was a suicide and not a murder. Still, my thoughts were hopelessly mixed and confused. I didn't tell the security guards who converged on the area that I knew Ruth's name. I left immediately. I didn't want the publicity. I felt a little ashamed that I was not forthcoming with more information about her and what she had told me before she committed suicide. I felt that perhaps the message she was trying to communicate, if I understood it correctly, should accompany any newspaper account of her suicide. I was certain without my intervention a photograph of that blood-splattered sign would never make it into the local newspaper. No one would want to tarnish the reputation of the city and its relationship to the international business community.

Maybe Ruth confided in me for a reason. Maybe she wanted me to be a messenger for her. Had I failed once again? Had another person looked to me for help and support, and I failed to provide it?

By the time I walked out of the bar, it was early evening and the sun was well behind the western horizon. The lights on the pier were on, and the sound of the ocean waves slapping against the concrete pilings that supported the pier were less aggressive and threatening.

I decided to walk to the end of the pier to see if A. C. was still there, or if he had left with his business associates. As I passed the tourist cottages, I could occasionally hear the hum of quiet voices. In other cottages, loud voices and laughter signaled a more boisterous, party-going group of tourists were the occupants.

There was no one at the end of the pier. It was completely empty. The darkness of the Pacific Ocean spread out into the western horizon and beyond. Unless A. C. was in one of the cottages I had just passed, he had gone someplace else with his associates from EWE International.

• • •

Ruth Morgan's bizarre suicide at the convention center intensified the anxieties I had felt since the day I witnessed the murder in the church rectory. The events of that day were never far from my mind, but after Ruth's suicide I found myself examining and reexamining even the smallest, seemingly most insignificant detail of what had happened that day in the rectory.

When I was in my apartment, I prayed for Ruth, asking God to help her troubled soul find some peace. I struggled with the prayer.

A wide chasm had opened up between me and the God I had worshipped since I was a boy. I struggled to see, or hear, if there was anyone on the other side of that chasm.

I also struggled to find a connection—any connection—between what had happened in the rectory and what had happened in the convention center. I could find no such connection.

When I was finally able to fall asleep, the nightmare came back with a vengeance—but with yet another twist. It started out the same way it always did, with Miranda walking into my office and sitting down to tell me her story, but it ended very differently after her husband rushed into the rectory.

Suddenly, the front door of the rectory burst violently open and smashed against the wall. A tall, bearded man with fierce, angry eyes rushed into the rectory. He was holding a pistol. When he saw his wife and me sitting in my office, he strode quickly across the foyer.

He paused for a moment in front of her. For a few precious seconds, I was frozen, unable to act. "No, Waldo!" Miranda screamed. "Don't do . . ."

As she held a hand up in the air to protect herself, her husband fired one shot into her head. She slumped to the floor and disappeared on the other side of the desk, while I remained seated.

Her husband stared at the pistol, seemingly not comprehending what he had just done. Then he looked at me. His eyes were vacant, puzzled. He looked down at the lifeless body of his wife, crumpled up on the floor. When he looked up again, the vacant, puzzled look in his eyes was gone. His eyes were once again filled with anger.

I closed my eyes, knowing what was going to come next. I waited for the explosion and the darkness that would follow. Instead, I heard frantic footsteps. When I opened my eyes, he was gone, and I was alone with his dead wife. . . .

This time it wasn't the collar that stopped him from killing me because I didn't have it on! It was something else that stopped him.

Did someone intercede on my behalf to stop him from killing me, too?

CHAPTER FOUR

decided to search more actively for some answers to the many questions that were haunting my obsessions and driving me away from the faith I had once embraced, but that now seemed grounded on such shifting, unstable soil. I felt like I needed to see the world as it really existed, through the eyes of those who had lost everything and merely struggled every day to survive. If they had anything left that sustained them in their darkest hours, I needed to know what it was, and how I, too, might find it. I thought I understood such suffering, but I didn't.

The next morning, I drove the van over to Grape Street and Ivy Avenue to see if I could find the foreclosed home Ruth Morgan told me she shared with other homeless people in that area. I was hoping some of them might be able to shed some light on her state of mind before she committed suicide at the International Business Forum. I needed to know if there were any connections to the two horrible deaths I had witnessed, and whether I was in some way responsible for either or both of them.

After I spotted the sign where Ivy Avenue and Grape Street intersected, I passed one abandoned home with windows and doors covered with plywood. Another home on that same street had a large foreclosed sign prominently displayed on the outer wall near the front windows. The yard of that home was covered with dead weeds.

I parked the van, walked up to the front porch, and knocked on the door. Moments later, I heard some muffled footsteps inside the house. Then there was silence.

"I'm one of Ruth Morgan's friends," I yelled, hoping that would relieve any concerns Ruth's fellow illegal occupants might have about a stranger knocking on the door. "I'm not with the bank or the police department. I was hoping to talk to you about Ruth."

The door scraped open an inch or two, but I could not see who was looking at me from the other side.

"I knew Ruth Morgan," I explained. "I was at the convention center when she killed herself."

The door scrapped open wider, and a middle-aged man, wearing worn and stained dress pants and shirt and shoes that looked like he had pulled them out of a dumpster, stared out at me. He studied me suspiciously. "Come in," he said finally.

He opened the door even wider, glanced quickly down the street in both directions, and stepped back inside. As soon as I walked into the house, he shut the door and turned the deadbolt into the locked position.

"My name is Philip Walker," he said, turning and extending a weathered palm in my direction.

"I'm Justin Moore," I said as I shook his hand. "I was a parish priest. Ruth was one of our volunteers. I ran into Ruth at the IBF convention and spoke to her briefly. Later, she committed suicide on the convention floor. I was hoping maybe you could help me understand what was going on with her."

"Probably the same thing that's going on with all of us," he said.

He led me into a living room where a woman and two young children were sitting on a badly stained mattress that looked like it had been pulled out of some back alley. There was no other furniture in the room.

"This is my wife Dorothy and our children, Annie and Ben," he said. "There were others living here, but they left this morning. With all the publicity surrounding Ruth's suicide, they figured the police would evict us today. They left to find another place for us to live." He gestured around the room. "I would offer you a chair," he said, "but as you see, we have no chairs."

"I don't need to sit. I won't be staying long."

"We were shocked when we heard what happened at the convention center," he said. "Ruth told us she was going there to protest the home foreclosures and job losses. We had no idea she planned to take her own life."

"Did she tell you anything else that might have motivated her to commit suicide at the IBF convention?"

"No. Nothing at all."

"The last thing she said to me was something like, 'It was supposed to be you. I just couldn't do it.' Did she ever mention my name to either of you?"

Philip shook his head. "I'm just at a loss to explain . . ."

"Philip," his wife interrupted him, "tell him about the voices."

"Maybe you should," he replied. "You were the one who talked to her about that."

"What voices?" I asked.

"She told me she'd been hearing voices," Dorothy said. "They've been telling her to do something more dramatic. Something to catch the attention of the media. She insisted that none of us should have to live like this."

"I had this feeling that she was giving up," Phillip said. "That's the only thing I saw in her that changed."

"She did say she talked to someone who had been following her," Dorothy added. "They told her there might be a long-term solution to what we're going through."

"Did she say who they were?" I asked.

"No," Dorothy said. "She was mostly pretty guarded about it. She seemed afraid of something. I'm not sure what. I'm not even sure she did talk to someone. She might have imagined the whole thing. I do remember one thing she said that didn't sound like the way she usually talked. She said, 'It feels like some kind of epic battle is being fought by economic giants and the rest of us are caught in the middle.' I thought at the time that it was pretty sophisticated talk. It sounded like she was quoting someone."

Suddenly, in the distance, we heard the sound of sirens.

"That could be them now!" Philip said. He walked over to the window and lifted a sun-bleached shade. "We keep moving from abandoned home to abandoned home, but they always catch up with us." He pushed the shade back against the window and turned to me. "You'd better get going. We just go out the back door and disappear into one of the canyons whenever they show up, but your car's out front. You probably should leave. They can evict us rather quickly once the landlord hires an attorney."

I quickly pulled out a notebook and pen from my shirt pocket and scribbled my address on a piece of paper. "This is where I live," I said, handing it to him. "Let me know what happens to your family."

• • •

A police car pulled up next to me as soon as I parked the van by my apartment. One of the officers who had taken me to the San Diego Police Headquarters rolled down the passenger widow. "Tindal wants to see you again," he said.

I obediently opened the door and slid into the back seat. Minutes later, we drove into the underground parking structure of the police headquarters and took the elevator up to one of the inter-rogation rooms on the third floor.

Tindal entered moments later, opened a file he was holding, and tossed a photograph of A. C. on the table in front of me. "So who is he?" he demanded to know, jabbing his index finger at the photograph.

"I have no idea," I replied.

"You've driven him to just about every tourist trap in this city, and you still don't know who he is?" he said angrily.

"Sounds like you've been following me again."

"Of course, we've been following you. Did you expect that we wouldn't?"

"Then you know as much about him as I do. He meets with strange people, all dressed in business suits. That's all I know about him."

"He has revealed nothing to you about who he represents?" Tin-dal insisted.

"No. He just says he's researching new business opportunities. He's very evasive."

"Think he's into drugs?"

"No, I don't. . . ."

"Art thief? Part of some nut case fringe group plotting to over-throw the government? A foreign terrorist organization infiltrating our county?"

"Maybe he's a legitimate businessman," I said. "Have you ever thought of that possibility?"

"Not when he works for a company that doesn't exist."

"Maybe he's with the CIA?"

Tindal was obviously puzzled by my comment. "Why do you bring them up?" he asked.

"Everyone he met was dressed the way I imagined high-level intelligence agents might dress. I immediately thought of the CIA."

Tindal pondered the possibility. "I don't think so. It's something else." He opened the file he was holding, pulled out another photo-graph, and slapped it on the table in front of me. "Here's something else. A photographer took this picture of you at the IBF convention."

It was a picture of me standing on the edge of a group of people moments after Ruth Morgan committed suicide. Most of the other people in the photograph had dropped to the floor.

"What about it?" I asked.

"I think you know what happened. A woman killed herself on the convention floor, and you were there."

"So were a lot of other people."

"They all stayed around to answer questions about what happened. You didn't, even though you were an eyewitness."

"No, I didn't stay," I agreed.

"How come?"

"Probably because I wanted to avoid having to come down here again and be pelted with questions for which I have no answers."

"Wherever you go, people seem to die," Tindal said, looking me directly in the eye. "You witness a murder in a church rectory. You live across the hall from another person who drowned in the bathtub. The next occupant of that same apartment is murdered. You interact with a homeless man in Balboa Park, and he dies. Then you are an eyewitness to a suicide at the convention center. People don't last very long after they've been around you. That doesn't sound like coincidence to me. It sounds like a trail of circumstantial evidence that you, and the person you work for, are involved in some kind of criminal activity."

● ● ●

I jogged over to Balboa Park later that day. I searched the many nooks and crannies of the park, trying to find Ilsa. I walked past the huge concrete enclosure that contained the Lily Pond and finally located her near the Alcazar Garden. As I made my way through the maze-like pathways, I saw that she was cutting small clippings off one of the Pittas Porum bushes and placing them in small plastic bags.

"You disappeared rather quickly the other day," I said, walking up to her.

"You were sound asleep," she said, looking up and smiling. "I didn't want to wake you."

"Did you figure out what it was that scared you that night?"

"I think it was a bad dream. I've been worrying too much about the bees."

"Have you figured out what's happening to them?"

"Not yet." She studied the bush and cut off another small branch. "What about you?"

"*What* about me?"

"You haven't told me what you do for a living?"

"Think you're ready for that?"

"Well, unless you're a homicidal maniac, or you've just escaped from a mental hospital, I think I can deal with it."

"What if it's worse than both of those possibilities?"

She laughed softly and said, "Then I shouldn't be standing here talking to you. I should be running for help."

"Actually, it's not all that exciting. I pick up odd jobs wherever I can find them."

"Surely you haven't been doing that all your life."

"No. I haven't."

"Then, tell me who you are and what you've been doing all your life? You don't look like the odd-job type to me."

"Okay, but I warned you."

"I can handle the truth."

"I'm a priest."

"Really?"

She looked up from the bush she was clipping and stared at me as though she was seeing me for the first time.

"Yes. But I'm not a priest any longer . . . or at least I'm on a leave of absence."

"Why?"

"Are you sure you want to know?"

"I spent the night with you," she replied teasingly. "Surely, I have the right to know why you are no longer a priest."

"You slept on the bed, and I slept on the floor," I corrected her.

"I know. But any woman who spends a night in the same apartment with a priest has the right to know why he is no longer one."

"I witnessed a murder in the rectory. An angry husband came in and killed his wife. I saw it all."

"Why would that cause you to leave the priesthood?" she asked, puzzled.

"I had time to stop it, and I didn't. I was more concerned about my own life than hers. That convinced me it was time to step back and see if I really belonged in the priesthood."

"I've seen you with that man in the wheelchair."

"I drive his van. It's my newest odd job."

"Who is he?"

"I don't know," I admitted. "No one seems to know."

"Isn't it kind of strange to work for someone you know nothing about?"

"Yes, I suppose it is."

Ilsa placed the clippers in a leather holster clipped to her belt. "If no one knows anything about him," she said, "doesn't it seem like maybe you could be getting yourself involved in something dangerous?"

"It certainly felt that way yesterday."

"What happened?"

"I witnessed another murder . . . well, actually a suicide."

"Another one?"

"Yes. One of the police detectives says wherever I go, someone seems to die."

"Why are you telling me all this?"

I paused to choose my words carefully. "I just wanted to put it all out on the table, in case maybe you would like to go out to supper with me some night. I don't think you would be in any danger, but I thought you should know."

"Are you asking me out on a date?"

"I'm technically still a priest, so we wouldn't have to think of it as a date."

"I accept. Since we've already spent a night in the same apartment, I guess going out to supper is not such a big deal."

• • •

When I returned from my jog the next morning, there was a folded note wedged into the door jamb of my apartment. I assumed it was probably from Ilsa, since we had agreed to go out to supper but had not agreed on a day or time. When I unfolded the note, I saw that it was signed by Philip Walker. In scrawled, shaky handwriting, he wrote, "We are holding a simple memorial service today for Ruth Morgan at 12 noon. We will be at 1923 Ivy Street. Please join us if you can."

I quickly showered, changed clothes, and walked outside to A. C.'s van. As I drove over to Ivy Street, I passed several vacant and foreclosed homes before I spotted the numbers 1923 above the front porch of an older, Victorian-style home that was badly in need of a paint job. A large foreclosed sign had been staked into the weed-strewn front yard.

The boards on the porch creaked and groaned under my weight as I walked up to the front door. Small mounds of termite droppings were evident next to one of the white guardrails. I knocked and waited until Dorothy Walker cautiously opened the door. When she saw it was me, she opened the door wider and gestured for me to step inside.

"I got your husband's note," I explained.

She nodded and escorted me into an adjacent room where an informal memorial service was already taking place. Philip Walker was standing on the fireplace hearth, speaking to a small group of other apparently homeless people who were sitting on the floor. There was no furniture in the room, so I sat down among them.

"We have learned that Ruth is to be cremated," Philip said to the group. "Since she has no family, her ashes will be scattered in a common grave. I believe Ruth killed herself to call attention to the plight of all of us. She sacrificed herself in the hope that others, like my children Annie and Ben, could live in a world less dominated by greed. I must confess to all of you that I was once a part of that world. I once thought the Ruth Morgans of the world were crazy. From the tenth floor of my office building, I looked down on them with contempt. That was before I, too, was laid off. Now I no longer feel that way. Ruth opened my eyes. So we are here today to honor Ruth in the only way we can, and that is for each of us to say a few words about her and what she meant to us."

Philip stepped off the fireplace hearth and joined the people sitting on the floor. His wife Dorothy immediately took his place at the front of the small gathering. "Ruth loved children," she said. "The death of her own daughter is what turned her into an activist for the poor and the homeless. She said it was difficult for her at first because she was raised to respect authority and the law. But as she saw more and more people lose their homes and jobs, or die because they were denied life-sustaining health care, she took to the streets. She said it was not something she ever expected to do. She thought she would have a quiet retirement. All of that was taken away from her. When she took her life in such a public way, she made one final protest on behalf of all those who are less fortunate. If any of us knew that she planned to take her own life, I am sure we would have tried to talk her out of it. So we can only feel gratitude for what she tried to do for us."

As Dorothy stepped down from the fireplace hearth, an elderly man with a long, white beard and dark, suntanned face replaced her at the front of the room. "There was a side to Ruth that many of you did not know," he said. "She was a deeply religious person. No, make that a deeply spiritual person. She was convinced the world was coming to an end. She said all of the signs from the Bible were there. She said the tidal wave of greed was predicted. She also said the poor will someday triumph, but their lives still need to be made bearable in this world. I did not share her religious beliefs. However, I did respect her passion and her commitment to helping the poorest of the poor have better lives. Let us all hope that the sacrifice she made in the convention center will not be forgotten."

As the elderly man sat down, the people sitting on the floor cast nervous glances at one another. When no one stood up to speak, Dorothy looked in my direction. "We have someone with us today," she said, "who knew Ruth before the many tragedies in her life sent her our way. Perhaps he would like to say a few words about her."

I stood and somewhat reluctantly walked over to the fireplace hearth. "My name is Justin Moore," I began. "I am on leave from the priesthood. Ruth was a volunteer in my parish. I knew her as one of the most able and industrious people I had ever met. Right now, I drive a van for a wheelchair-bound businessman who works for a large international corporation. I was at the convention center with him when it happened. I talked to Ruth briefly before she took her own life. I wasn't expecting her to commit suicide. It came as a complete surprise. She held up a sign with the words, 'The IBF is a den of thieves.' Then she kept repeating, 'They killed my daughter, and now they're killing me.' I didn't know what to make of all that. I still don't. I wish I had more to tell you. I wish I had known what she was planning to do so I could have tried to talk her out of it."

There were others in the group who spoke after me, but I was lost in my thoughts and did not listen to them very closely. After the memorial service, I gestured for Dorothy to follow me into an adjacent room. "The last time we talked," I said, "you mentioned that Ruth was hearing voices before she died. Did she ever say what kind of voices she was hearing?"

"All she told me was that she noticed some people were following her. She figured they were from the FBI or some other government agency. She figured they were keeping an eye on her because of her political activism. After that, she started hearing the voices. I didn't know what to make of it at the time. Then a couple of days ago, I was going through an old purse she left behind the day she went to the International Business Forum. She had scribbled a bunch of notes and messages across the pages of a notebook. From what I could gather, she was able to see someone at the People's Clinic, which is a mental health clinic for the poor and homeless.

Ruth wrote down the word 'schizophrenia' on the notebook. So it's possible that came up during her meeting there."

"Did she say *who* she met with at the clinic?" I asked.

"No," Dorothy replied. "She noted that there had been cuts in the clinic's budget, and they couldn't see her again. They also expressed concerns that they were running out of funding and might have to close the clinic."

"Did they close it?"

"Yes. It was closed the day Ruth committed suicide."

"Maybe that's why she did it," I speculated.

"That or the people she said were following her," Dorothy speculated softly. "Maybe they talked her into doing it. They might have been very real in her mind."

"Do you still have the notebook?"

"No. I had to leave it behind when we made a quick escape into the canyon after we heard a police siren. Either they have it or whoever cleaned up after us probably threw it out."

"Did Ruth ever say how the people in her dreams were dressed?" I asked.

"No, she said nothing about that."

"Did she say what the voices were telling her?"

"The only thing I remember her saying is that 'good and evil often look the same.' I don't know why she said it, or what she was referring to."

• • •

Was Ruth Morgan schizophrenic, and that was why she killed herself? Or was she actually hearing real voices that told her to do something she did not want to do? Something that apparently involved me. So she killed herself rather than do it.

I didn't know the answers to those questions, but I decided if A. C. and the people I had seen him with were involved in any way, perhaps I could find some answers in his apartment.

My apartment manager, whose name I had never learned, was a slovenly man with a potbelly and huge red nose who spent most of his time drinking cheap wine. He rarely came out of his apartment, unless it was to attend to something so important it simply could not be ignored. Even then, he rarely fixed anything properly. He made superficial repairs of leaky pipes, plugged sinks, or dripping faucets—and then he would immediately disappear back into his apartment.

I was hoping, however, that his vices might work in my favor. If I asked him for the key to A. C.'s apartment, he might be too lazy and inebriated to accompany me to the third floor. With A. C. absent, I wanted to see if there was anything up there that might tell me more about my mysterious employer. I speculated that he might be somehow connected to the many bizarre circumstances in my life, even the death of Ruth Morgan. I don't know why I came to that conclusion. It was just something I felt in the depths of my own troubled soul.

I knocked on the manager's door, and he soon appeared. As usual, he looked like he'd been drinking most of the day. "I'm Justin," I said. "From down the hall."

"I know who you are," he mumbled.

"I wonder if you could help me. I've been driving a van for the resident who lives in Room 312—"

"I've seen the two of you leave the building together," he said, interrupting me.

"He left town for a few days, and he asked me to service the van and run a few errands for him. He apparently left the keys in his apartment. I have no way of getting in there."

"I'm not sure I can do that."

"He's going to need the van as soon as he gets back," I insisted.

The manager studied me for a few moments. Then he reached for a set of keys hanging from a hook on the inside wall and handed them to me. "I'd go with you," he said," but I'm a little under the weather today. Just return these as soon as you're done up there."

I thanked him and walked over to the elevator, which was located around the corner from the mailboxes. I pushed the button on the control panel and listened to the ancient elevator rumble and groan as it descended from the second floor. Once I stepped into the elevator and the door closed behind me, the rumbling and groaning noises were almost painful to the ears.

When I got out on the third floor, it was suddenly very quiet. There wasn't a sound anywhere. I inserted the key into the lock on room 312, turned it counterclockwise, and opened the door. When I stepped into the apartment, my immediate impression was that it looked like it was vacant. As I explored the individual rooms, I realized there were no clothes in the closet, no food in the refrigerator, no dishes or eating utensils in the cupboards. There was a kitchen table and two chairs, but no salt and pepper shakers, place mats, or napkins that indicated it had ever been used for a single meal. There was a bed with one pillow, but there were no sheets or blankets. There was no evidence in any of the rooms that anyone even lived in the apartment. It reminded me of my former neighbor's apartment the day I heard a noise and found Tindal inspecting it.

Who are these people? How can they live like this?

The only piece of furniture that seemed to have any function whatsoever was a folding table in the living room with a laptop computer on it. The computer was in the sleep mode, but as I pressed one of the keys on the keyboard a screensaver quickly appeared on the monitor. The stars and other celestial bodies streaked across the screen in bright, radiant colors.

For a few seconds, I watched the stars dance across the monitor. Then I took another look around the room. Before leaving, I pulled a piece of paper out of my notebook, crumpled it into a small ball, and inserted it into the door lock so I could reenter the apartment without having to ask the manager for the key again. I pulled the door shut and glanced at the numbers 312 at the top of the wooden door panel.

How, I wondered, could he live up here without any way of cooking or eating? He couldn't possibly get to any of the local restaurants in his wheelchair.

Who is he?

CHAPTER FIVE

started the next day with my usual jog to the big fountain in Balboa Park. I had hoped to connect with Ilsa to talk about our dinner plans, but another park employee told me she was working in an area that was closed to the public. So while I soaked in the sunshine and drank my coffee, I continued to contemplate what I had seen in A. C.'s apartment the previous evening. Unless he was some kind of monk who had adopted an extremely ascetic lifestyle, there seemed to be only one reason for him to live so frugally.

If he has to get out of town quickly, for any reason whatsoever, all he would have to do is grab the laptop computer and leave. There is nothing else he would have to worry about because there is nothing else in the apartment to take with him.

Still, I was not convinced that it was possible for anyone confined to a wheelchair to live without food, clothing, and the other basic necessities of life at his immediate disposal.

It has to be something else. But what?

I watched as a long string of wheelchairs carrying small children emerged from the parking lot behind the San Diego Natural History Museum. It moved slowly, steadily along a concrete walkway. As they approached the area where I was sitting, I saw that adult caretakers were pushing some physically and mentally challenged children toward the San Diego Aerospace Museum, and probably toward the playground area farther south.

Some of the children's heads were arched backwards, as though they were staring at the cloud formations high overhead. Others had slumped down in their wheelchairs until their chins rested on their chests. Still others had fallen asleep, and their heads leaned so far to the left or right, they seemed to be resting on their shoulders.

When they passed the area where I was sitting, a young boy and girl rolled their eyes in my direction and struggled to smile through lips that were either partially paralyzed or deformed from some accident or birth defect. Other children, who were apparently brain damaged or the victims of neurological diseases, struggled to walk alongside the wheelchair-bound children while the caretakers stood close by, steadying them so they did not trip and fall onto the concrete walkway.

I continued to watch the caravan of youthful, broken bodies until it disappeared behind the aerospace museum. Then some of the doubts and questions I had been struggling with in my own life rushed over me like an angry tide crashing against a rock-covered shoreline.

How can this happen to innocent children? They did nothing to deserve their fates. Yet their entire lives would be one long, endless struggle just to breathe and feed themselves.

In my own troubled state of mind, it was too much to think about. So I decided not to think about it anymore.

As I surveyed the other people walking in the park, I caught a glimpse of a banner advertising the "Renaissance Art Exhibition" on a pole near the fountain. I remembered that A. C. had demonstrated a keen interest in the Renaissance paintings on display, and I wondered if perhaps it would be worth my time to pay a return visit to the museum. I also did not get a good look at the adjacent room where he had discussed his plans with someone in unusually cryptic and ambiguous language.

I walked over to the museum of art, paid the entrance fee, and made my way to the exhibit rooms in the rear of the first floor. Once again, there were security personnel and guides standing on guard along the hallway and in each of the exhibit rooms. I wandered slowly around the room where I had waited for A. C., studying the intricate details in the many Renaissance paintings of royal families, biblical subjects, various renditions of the crucifixion of Christ, and other beautifully designed and intricately executed paintings. I paused by Da Vinci's drawing, *Study of the Madonna*, and two Raphael portraits of aristocratic women, one titled *Lady with a Unicorn* and the other *Portrait of a Woman*. Then I walked over to the exhibit monitor who was standing just inside the doorway.

"I have kind of a strange question," I said.

"We don't consider any question too strange to answer," he replied politely.

"These paintings," I said, gesturing with both hands at the paintings hanging on the walls, "they must be incredibly valuable."

"Yes, indeed, they are."

"How do they transport them all the way to this country without damaging them? I would think that would be a major undertaking."

"It is," he agreed. "But there are companies that are experienced in those matters. They know exactly how to pack and store them. Only highly trained professionals are allowed to have anything to do with their transportation. These paintings are, of course, irreplaceable."

"Is one of those companies EWE International?" I asked.

"How do you spell it?"

"EWE . . . like a female sheep."

"No, I have never heard of a company by that name in the art business."

I could tell that he was becoming a little suspicious of my questions, so I decided to change the subject. "I've read about these Renaissance painters," I said. "Da Vinci, Michelangelo, and the others. They were such geniuses."

"Yes, indeed they were."

"They seem almost to be some higher form of humanity."

"They were that, too," he agreed.

"Yet, they came into the world in a cluster, almost at the same time. That seems very unusual."

"They were surrounded by great artistic traditions," he explained. "They fed off those traditions. I suppose that's the great mystery of genius. Where does it come from?"

He excused himself and walked over to observe a group of people who had just wandered into the exhibit room. Before leaving, I decided to visit the adjacent room to see where A. C. and his business acquaintance had met to discuss their plans.

The room contained more Renaissance paintings from the same artists I had already observed, and also some works by less famous artists. At a glance, the paintings hanging on the walls in that room seemed to reflect a darker, more cynical view of human life. The crucifixion scenes were more violent and savage. A few scenes from the *Book of Revelation* revealed in gory detail the fate of all sinners on the Judgment Day. Albrecht Durer's woodcut, *The Four Horsemen of the Apocalypse,* was in the middle of one of the walls, surrounded by other biblical subjects and some portraits of Renaissance aristocrats.

There was nothing unusual about the room itself. It appeared to be a planned meeting place for A. C. and a business associate, nothing more. Still, I remembered their strange conversation as though it were taking place right where I was standing.

"So where are we in all of this?" the man asked.

"It is not time yet," A. C. replied. *"It would be premature."*
"If not now, when?"
"When everything is in place. It all takes time."
"Time is not something we have a lot of."
"I know they are impatient."
"They may not wait much longer."
"Maybe I will have to go back and try to convince them it is in their best interests to wait."
"You may have to do that."

They had communicated with one another in what seemed to be a coded language. Anyone who overheard them couldn't possibly understand what they were trying to say—or what important decision they, or someone they knew, would be making in the near future.

I had no idea what it all meant.

On my way out of the museum, I passed a group of tourists milling about in a souvenir shop and bookstore. As I approached the turnstile on the exit side of the ticket booth, a muscular, middle-aged man with a security badge pinned to his suit greeted me.

"Thank you for coming," he said. "Have a nice day."

I thought I heard something vaguely familiar in his voice. After passing through the turnstile, I stepped off to the side and pretended to be waiting for someone while I listened to him give similar greetings to three more people. What was vaguely familiar about his voice became more obvious with each person who passed through the turnstile.

I did hear that voice before. He's the person I overheard A. C. speaking to in the adjacent exhibit room.

• • •

For the rest of the day, I twisted my imaginary Rubik's Cube in every possible way, trying to determine what patterns would align themselves on any one of the six sides of the puzzle. Nothing worked to create a single, irrefutable pattern. Only one possibility tied most of the seemingly isolated incidents into a plausible alignment.

Maybe Tindal is right. Maybe A. C. is an international art thief. Maybe he is planning to steal some of the art treasures that are currently on display in the museum of art.

Many things certainly pointed in that direction. He obviously had a business relationship with one of the security people at the art museum, and they discussed plans to pull off some kind of inside job. A. C. was also well versed in art history and had even displayed a significant artistic talent in the pencil drawing he left behind in the van. The people he met in the blue business suits and reconnected with at the International Business Forum also did not seem like common thieves, as might be the case if he was working for a drug cartel. They seemed instead to be the type of sophisticated, well-positioned businessmen and women who might have the necessary connections to help him sell the stolen art treasures in the international black market. Furthermore, the warehouse we visited the first day I drove the van might be the perfect place to hide the art treasures until they could be smuggled out of the country.

Whatever the case, A. C. was certainly not what he claimed to be: an accountant for a legitimate international business looking for new investment opportunities in the San Diego area. If he was an accountant, he was unlike any other accountant I had ever met. Accountants keep books and work quietly behind the scenes. They are not the point men who search for new markets for whatever products or services a business is trying to sell. An accountant is a numbers manager. They keep or inspect financial accounts. They are not marketing people.

A. C.'s superficial attempts to pass himself off as an accountant were clearly intended to conceal his true identity—and that identity appeared to be international art thief. No legitimate business person working for an international company lived in a run-down apartment with nothing in the way of personal possessions except for a single computer. They rented luxury suites in Downtown hotels, where everything was provided for them and they were treated like royalty.

Did that mean I was complicit in a crime that had not yet been committed? Was it time for me to go to Tindal with what I knew, or at least suspected?

About the only thing that did not fit in the emerging pattern involving a possible international art theft was A. C.'s request to visit the section of San Diego with the greatest number of homeless people. Unless he was meeting with an accomplice who was deeply buried in the bowels of the city, far beneath the work-a-day world of the more respectable Downtown businesses, it simply did not fit into the emerging pattern.

Maybe he was exploring another place to hide the stolen art treasures, at least temporarily. Maybe that's all it was.

In the days that followed, I checked the bulletin board every morning to see if there was a note from A. C. announcing that he had returned from his business trip and would need my services again. Every morning the bulletin board was empty except for the usual scribbled notes from tenants who had something they wanted to sell, either to support their addictions or to put food on their tables.

In the meantime, I twisted my imaginary Rubik's Cube into every possible pattern, while I pondered whether I should continue to drive A. C.'s van, or bail before I found myself overwhelmed by powerful international forces far beyond my ability to comprehend or resist.

• • •

Ilsa and I finally agreed on a time to have supper together. We met in the hallway between our two apartments and drove over to the Old Town Mexican Café. We parked the van near some restored historic structures that had once constituted San Diego's main street. We settled into a booth and ate chips and salsa while a Mariachi band played on the back patio.

"How's it going with your new employer?" she asked as we waited for our food.

"I still don't know what to make of him," I admitted. "But I think he might be into something illegal."

"Like what?"

"He might be an international art thief."

"You have evidence of that?" she asked, clearly surprised.

"Nothing concrete. But I'm worried that he and his associates could be planning to steal some of the art works on display in the museum of art in Balboa Park."

"Shouldn't you be going to the police if you think that's going to happen?"

She was clearly surprised by my rather nonchalant attitude toward what might be a planned heist of some of the world's greatest art treasures.

"I haven't had good luck with the police," I explained. "I'm not sure what they'd make of my suspicions. I'm just thinking of giving up my job as his driver."

"Shouldn't you—"

"Let's not talk about that anymore," I said, gently interrupting her. "This is a night to relax, not talk about my job. Besides, I've been wanting to talk to you about something else. I need a scientist's advice."

"I'm more of a bug collector than a scientist."

"I've been over to the Renaissance painting exhibit in Balboa Park. I've also been reading about the great geniuses that came out of that time period. . . ."

"Sounds like you need an art historian more than a scientist," she said.

"No. You'll do just fine. What I've been trying to figure out is how do you get a cluster of geniuses like Da Vinci, Michelangelo, and the other Renaissance masters who came into the world about the same time? I can see it happening randomly, but not in clusters."

"Like I said, I'm a bug collector, not a geneticist."

"Certainly you've studied evolution."

"Of course."

"From what I know, evolutionary change takes place over many, many years. Even centuries. Yet, there are those periodic spikes when geniuses like Michelangelo and Da Vinci suddenly propel the human race into a whole new dimension. A whole new way of looking at human life. How do scientists account for that?"

"I'm not sure they can," she replied. "Everything is determined at the moment of conception. I suppose there will be some conceptions when the perfect sperm comes together with the perfect egg—and you get a genius. Then you can also have the opposite effect, when something goes very wrong at the moment of conception, and the child is handicapped for life."

"I saw a caravan of those children in the park recently," I said. "I guess that's why all of this is on my mind."

"I saw them, too," she replied. "But like I said, I'm not a geneticist. I'm more of a bug collector than a scientist. Right now, I'm trying to figure out what's killing the bees in this area."

"Have you had any luck?"

"Maybe. Have you ever heard of chemicals like Acetamiprid, Clothianidin, Dinotefuran, Imidaclorprid, or Thiamethoxam?"

"I couldn't even pronounce the names," I admitted, "much less know what they are."

"They're used in all kinds of insecticides and other products. They're certainly some of the primary suspects for what's killing off the bees."

"There are other suspects, too?" I asked.

"We can't account for everything that's happening to the bees. We only know that the deaths of the colonies, if they continue, could prove to be far more threatening to human life than just about any other kind of manmade or natural catastrophe. It could wipe out our food sources, and millions would die from starvation. It could even trigger one of those extinction events the world has suffered through many times before. Some people have even speculated that it might be deliberate."

"Why would anyone do that?"

"Whoever controls the world's food supplies controls the world," she explained.

"That would be about as ruthless as it gets," I said.

"Yes, it would," she agreed. "But it's not unheard of. Tyrants throughout history have practiced such genocide on their enemies, and sometimes their own people. Starvation is a powerful weapon."

• • •

Before we said goodnight, Ilsa invited me to join her the next day. She said she was going to do some research on the ocean side of the Point Loma Peninsula. She wanted to determine if the die-off of the bee colonies was as severe in that area as it was in Balboa Park. She said that information might give her a clue as to whether the same thing was affecting the bee populations elsewhere in the area. If not, she might be able to isolate the source of the die-off in Balboa Park.

Early the next morning, I accompanied her as she drove a work van over to Point Loma's commercial area and turned west on a winding road through the foothills. When we entered the Fort Rosecrans National Cemetery, I noticed thousands of white military headstones arranged in neat rows on both sides of the road. As we approached the end of the peninsula, we could see the Pacific Ocean spread out into the western horizon. In the east, the Downtown San Diego skyscrapers towered into the sky.

Ilsa turned west onto a much narrower dirt road and followed it along a steep hillside. After we parked halfway down the hillside, we got out and she opened the trunk and pulled out a backpack. She slipped her arms into the canvas straps and adjusted it to her shoulders.

"There's a trail over there," she said, pointing at a narrow dirt path that followed the contours of the peninsula in a southerly direction. "We have to follow it for about a quarter of a mile."

We proceeded to walk along the trail until Ilsa suddenly stopped and pointed at a weathered concrete bunker embedded in the hillside.

"Know what that is?" she asked.

"No."

"It's a World War II bunker," she explained. "The military was expecting a Japanese invasion. They built a number of these bunkers along this hillside."

I paused and tried to peer inside the narrow slit facing the ocean side of the concrete bunker, but the weeds were too thick.

"Fortunately," Ilsa continued, "the Japanese never invaded this country, although they considered it. So our military never had to use these bunkers."

We walked past the bunker and soon encountered some thick bushes that had overgrown the trail. Dead bees covered the ground at the base of the bushes.

"It's spreading," she said.

"What is?" I asked.

"Whatever is killing the bees is spreading."

She put a rubber glove on her right hand, picked up several of the bees, and placed them in a plastic container she pulled out of the backpack. She sighed deeply and looked out over the Pacific Ocean as though expecting the World War II Japanese battleships and destroyers to suddenly appear on the horizon.

• • •

Later that morning, we returned to the World War II bunker and sat down to eat some sandwiches Ilsa pulled out of her backpack. We leaned against the crumbling concrete wall and stared out at the Pacific Ocean while we ate the sandwiches and enjoyed the ocean breeze.

"So what do you think of what we found back there?" I asked.

"Nothing good. Whatever is killing the bees appears to be doing it regionwide."

"Still think it's those chemicals you mentioned last night?"

"Possibly. But if it is, the use of the chemicals is far more widespread than I thought."

"How long have you been doing this kind of work?" I asked. "You've never told me much about yourself."

"What do you need to know?"

"Where you came from? What you did before you came out here?"

"There's not much to tell," she said somewhat evasively.

"Try me."

"My family is from Hungary, but I was born in this country. Not much out of the ordinary ever happened to me, although I almost drowned once. A stranger saved me. I grew up in the East, had plans to become a doctor. Nothing I planned worked out. Little by little, I ended up out here. Things just kept happening to me. Things I didn't see coming."

"Sounds like my life," I admitted. "I certainly never thought I would be an ex-priest, working at odd jobs, and living in a cheap apartment while I tried to figure out what to do with my life."

"Sometimes I guess life is just what happens to us. Not what we choose to do with it."

"Maybe."

"Or maybe it's just one small accident after another," she speculated, "until we end up someplace we never thought we'd be."

"Like an ex-priest who finds himself sitting next to a crumbling, abandoned World War II bunker, looking out over the Pacific Ocean and eating lunch with an entomologist who studies and collects dead bees for a living?"

"I guess you didn't see that one coming, did you?" she replied, laughing gently.

"No, I didn't," I admitted.

• • •

We spent a few more hours combing the hillside, looking for dead or dying bees. The evidence of die-offs was everywhere. Many hives were abandoned, and mounds of dead bees littered the trailside. Ilsa filled all of her specimen containers. Finally, she decided it was time for us to leave. After we walked back to the van, she threw the backpack into the trunk.

We paused to gaze out over the Pacific Ocean and feel the ocean breeze one more time before leaving. Then I turned to walk around to the passenger side of the vehicle. Suddenly, on the hillside above us, I spotted two men in dark business suits looking in our direction.

As Ilsa shut the trunk door, she noticed that my eyes were fixed on the two figures. "Know them?" she asked.

"No," I replied.

"Ever see them before?"

"Yes."

"Where?"

"I believe they're two of the people who met with A. C. when I was driving him around town."

"Are you sure?" she asked.

"They were all dressed that way."

"I think I've seen them before, too."

"Where?" I asked, looking at her.

"In Balboa Park. They just pop up somewhere unexpectedly. Moments later, they're gone. They seem a little strange to me."

When I looked at the top of the hillside again, both of the men had disappeared from sight.

• • •

On the way back from Point Loma, I tried to convince Ilsa to join me for a visit to A. C.'s third-floor apartment. She was reluctant to do so, and even tried to talk me out of it. However, I convinced her that A. C.'s business associates seemed to be unusually interested in Balboa Park, and perhaps in her research, and we needed to find out why. I told her we would quickly check out the apartment and then leave. After much coaxing, she finally agreed to accompany me.

I checked the bulletin board in the foyer to make sure there was no message from A. C. indicating he was back and would need me in the morning. Seeing that the bulletin board was empty, except for a few announcements from other tenants, we took the elevator up to the third floor. After the groaning and rumbling had stopped, we stepped out of the elevator and walked over to A. C.'s apartment. I pushed on the door, and it opened easily.

"What if he's here?" Ilsa whispered softly.

"He's not," I reassured her. "If he was back, he would have left a note for me on the bulletin board."

I shut the door behind us and checked the adjacent rooms to make certain we were alone. As I suspected, A. C. had not yet returned from his business trip.

"Are you sure he lives here?" Ilsa asked when I returned to the living room. "There's nothing in this apartment."

"I know," I said as I stepped behind the computer. "Come over here and see what you think of this."

"What of it?" she asked, joining me behind the computer.

I pressed the space bar on the keyboard, and the starburst screensaver filled the computer screen. "I was hoping you know enough about computers to get us into some of his personal files."

"It's locked," she said. "You would have to know the password to open it."

"Maybe he's a little sloppy with his computer security," I speculated. "Maybe the password is something obvious."

I proceeded to test several different passwords. I typed in the letters A. C., but they were rejected. The word accountant was also rejected. I tried a variety of other words that I associated with A. C., but none of them worked.

"You said he was interested in art history," Ilsa suggested. "Maybe you should try some words that are associated with art and artists."

I typed in the name Da Vinci, but it, too, was rejected. The word Raphael was also rejected. However, when I typed in the name Michelangelo, the word "Welcome" appeared on the screen.

"You're in," Ilsa said calmly.

We waited for what seemed like a long time for the welcome screen to disappear. Finally, it was replaced by the word MICHEL-ANGELO in large capital letters. We waited for it to disappear and be replaced by the main menu. Several minutes later, the word MICHELANGELO still lingered on the screen.

"Someone has reprogrammed this computer for their own personal use," Ilsa speculated. "There is no main menu. There is only a single menu under the name Michelangelo."

"Why would someone do something like that?"

"I suppose for greater security."

"Then how does one access it?"

"You don't. The only person who would be able to access it is the person who reprogrammed it. It would fit none of the normal conventions of computer use."

I stepped back and studied the screen. "There's a Michelangelo drawing in the recently opened Renaissance Art Exhibition," I said. "Do you think behind this password there is a detailed plan A. C. and his associates are putting in place to steal some of the Renaissance masterpieces?"

"It's possible," Ilsa agreed. "Maybe that's why those men I told you about are popping up everywhere in Balboa Park. They must be planning something over there."

"Might they also be testing something in this area that they plan to use later? Maybe in a more widespread attempt to kill off the bees and control the world's food sources, as you suggested earlier?"

"As a scientist, I never took those conspiracy theories seriously before," she admitted. "But now I'm beginning to wonder if there's something to them."

• • •

My thoughts later that evening were not on what Ilsa and I had discovered in A. C.'s apartment. They were on the caravan of wheelchair-bound children who had rolled past the area where I was sitting in Balboa Park. I could not get the thought out of my mind that their lives had virtually ended before they had a chance to begin. Most of them would never be able to do anything as simple as tie their own shoelaces or put a spoon to their mouths. Yet, there had to be a reason for bringing them into the world in such weak, fragile bodies.

In the museum of art, however, I wandered among art works created by the greatest geniuses the world had ever known. Everything Michelangelo, Da Vinci, and the other Renaissance masters touched was cloaked in the aura of their greatness. They had expanded our understanding of what it meant to be human, and they had pushed us a little closer to the Heavens.

How is it possible to reconcile a world in which such genius coexisted alongside the frail, sickly bodies of children who could not even walk? How can one reconcile such cruel injustices?

CHAPTER SIX

awaited A. C.'s return with mounting trepidation. So long as I was driving his van, I was connected to him and whatever secrets he had concealed in his computer. I considered leaving the van keys in his apartment with a note explaining that I would no longer be working as his driver. I quickly realized I would be unable to carry through with that decision because I would then have to explain how I got into his apartment. But it was something else that held me back. Something I did not understand or know how to resist. It was taking hold of my every thought, my every emotion.

• • •

One morning I parked the van near the St. Joseph's Catholic Church and walked inside to sit in one of the pews, while I meditated about the strange meandering path my life had taken. I couldn't shake the past. It kept coming back at me unexpectedly.

Is it time for me to end my leave of absence and go back to the life of a parish priest? Am I ready for that?

As I sat amidst the cool, early morning shadows and studied the biblical figures on the stained-glass windows, I realized they were imitations of Michelangelo's style.

It all started with him. He created the style that adorns many modern churches.

As I contemplated Michelangelo's profound influence on modern art and religious iconography, a bearded, apparently homeless man in a dirt-stained, red shirt wandered into the church and sat down on the other side of the aisle closer to the altar. Moments later, I stood and walked out of the church and past a pile of donated clothing in the rear vestibule.

Suddenly, I heard a strange noise behind me. When I turned to look back into the church, the homeless man in the red shirt was no longer sitting in one of the front pews. He had disappeared from sight. I assumed that after a rough night on the streets, he had probably slumped down in the pew to take a nap.

• • •

Another day passed, and still no note from A. C. on the bulletin board. I was beginning to question whether he had left the area for good. Perhaps, I speculated, he sensed that he was under surveillance and decided to leave San Diego for greener, more lucrative pastures. Then another thought occurred to me.

What if I am being set up to take the fall for whatever he is planning?

I was less convinced that A. C. worked for some ruthless international corporation that was determined to control the world's food sources, albeit that was still a possibility. I was far more convinced that whatever he was up to involved stolen art treasures that were to be resold on the black market.

If so, I was implicated in many different ways. I was connected to his white van. I had visited the Renaissance Art Exhibition with him and another time by myself. I had made my presence felt in the art museum by the questions I asked the exhibit monitor regarding the value of the paintings and drawings that were on display. I had stood in front of the Michelangelo drawing and studied it, while I marveled at how much it resembled A. C.'s drawing of the homeless people near the East Side Rescue Mission. I had also been in A. C.'s apartment and left my fingerprints all over his computer. I was everywhere in A. C.'s life since he arrived in San Diego.

If he committed a crime, how could I explain those connections? How convincing would I be if, after the crime, I told the authorities I didn't even know his name? I only knew his initials, A. C., an abbreviation for Accountant. Yet I continued to work as his driver. Would anyone believe I was not involved in the crime? Would the bishop abandon me or provide me with an attorney?

I had painted myself into a corner from which there was no escape.

No, that was the wrong analogy. I had created a pattern that pointed to the irrefutable conclusion that I was an accomplice in some kind of nefarious international crime.

I was so involved in contemplating the web of circumstantial evidence I had woven around myself that I didn't hear the soft knock on my apartment door. When my visitor knocked again, I assumed it was probably Ilsa, so I stood up and opened the door— and found myself looking at one of the officers who had driven me to the Downtown police headquarters before.

"Not again," I said.

• • •

At the police headquarters, the officer escorted me into a different interrogation room than the one I had visited previously. The room was larger, and it had an overhead projector and pull-down movie screen on the front wall. Moments later, Tindal and another detective walked into the room. Tindal's partner pulled the screen down across a small whiteboard with some faint, blue traces of a previous police update that had apparently been held in the room. Then he walked over to a computer keyboard that was partially concealed behind a small podium in one corner. I heard a steady humming sound emit from the overhead projector, and a bright light appeared on the pull-down screen.

"I have some surveillance footage I want to show you," Tindal said as he sat down on the opposite side of the table from me.

As I heard a clicking sound over by the computer, an image of a man walking up the concrete steps of the St. Joseph's Catholic Church appeared on the screen.

"Know who that is?" Tindal asked.

"It's me," I said.

"Remember what you were doing?"

"I was going to church."

"Why?"

"I go there to think. Remember, I am still a priest, even though I am on a leave of absence."

The image of a bearded man in a bright-red shirt soon appeared on the screen. He also walked up the steps and disappeared inside the church.

"Ever see him before?" Tindal asked.

"He walked into the church shortly after I did."

"What happened to him in there?"

"What do you mean?"

"Did he try to talk to you?"

"No. He sat down in another pew. I left almost as soon as he arrived."

"So you had no contact with him?"

"No. As I was leaving, I looked back and didn't see him any-more. . . . What's this all about?"

Tindal gestured to his partner, and the image on the screen im-mediately disappeared. The other detective turned off the overhead projector and walked out of the room.

"We found him this morning next to a dumpster in an alley near the church," Tindal said. "He was dead."

"Another one?"

"As I said before, you seem to attract them."

"I don't know what's going on," I said, the frustration clearly evident in my voice. "I have no idea what any of this means."

"We don't either," Tindal admitted. "But you seem to be a light-ning rod for a lot of unusual things that are happening in this city."

"I think they're somehow connected to A. C," I insisted. "But I don't know how they're connected."

"You still don't know what he's up to?"

"I think it has something to do with the Renaissance Art Exhibi-tion. They might be planning to steal some of those pieces that are on display in the museum of art. That's the only thing I've been able to come up with."

"We talked about that before," Tindal reminded me, "and you didn't think it had anything to do with stolen art works."

"I've changed my mind," I admitted.

"What caused you to change it?"

"A lot of things that can't be explained any other way."

"Does that include what you just saw up there?" Tindal asked, nodding in the direction of the pull-down screen at the front of the room.

"I don't know what to make of that. Or why people have been dy-ing around me. I only know that I'm going to tell A. C., whoever he might be, that I'm no longer going to drive his van. I want to extract myself from this mess before it's too late."

"We don't want you to do that," Tindal said calmly, but firmly.

"Do what?"

"Give up your job as his driver."

"Why?"

"Because we want you to keep an eye on his activities and re-port back to us what he's doing. We haven't been able to crack this nutshell with any of our own resources. We need you to report to us anything he does that's unusual."

"*Everything* he does is unusual."

"Then report it to us."

"And if I say no?"

"We'll still have you under surveillance, only you won't be working for us. You'll be working for him. Whatever comes out of this, if it ends up in an indictment and trial, you'll look much better as a witness for our side than an accomplice on his."

• • •

By the time the police officer dropped me off at my apartment, I was deeply troubled by the role Tindal had asked me to play in building a case against A. C. It was not so much a misguided sense of loyalty to my mysterious employer. It had more to do with my growing concern that I was being set up to take a fall, perhaps by A. C., or maybe by Tindal.

As I reflected on my suspicions, I remembered what Ruth Morgan had said in the days before she died. According to Dorothy Walker, Ruth told her, "Good and evil often look the same." Like Ruth, I didn't know which side I was on anymore.

When I stepped into my apartment, I had even more reason to be concerned. As soon as I opened the door, I noticed that many of my things had been moved and were out of place. The pillows on the bed had been pulled aside. The items that had piled up on top of the bookcase had been rearranged. Even my Rubik's Cube and the book I had placed facedown weeks earlier had been moved to a different corner of the end table next to my reading chair.

"Anything wrong?" Ilsa asked as she appeared in the doorway.

"Someone's been in here."

"Who?"

"I have no idea."

"Did they take anything?"

"I don't know. Things have been moved around. . . . I thought you worked today."

"I came back to see if you wanted to go with me to the Downtown library. I need to look up a few things on the flora and fauna in this area. . . . Are you sure nothing is missing in your apartment?"

"No, I think everything is here. I don't think it was a thief."

"Who was it then?" she asked.

"I think the detective who has me under surveillance lured me down to police headquarters so someone working for him could get into my apartment while I was gone."

"What do you think they were looking for?"

"Anything that would connect me to a lot of strange things that are happening in this city."

• • •

I decided to take Ilsa up on her offer. Ever since I had seen the word MICHELANGELO appear in bold, capital letters on A. C.'s computer screen, I thought that perhaps I should try to learn more about the great Renaissance artist. Perhaps something in Michelangelo's background would explain A. C.'s connection to him—*if* that connection involved anything more than a criminal mind trying to devise a plan to steal art treasures. Since Ilsa had provided me with the opportunity to learn more about Michelangelo, I decided to take advantage of it.

At the library, we went our separate ways. Ilsa wandered off to the floor where she said the books on native vegetation were stored. I took the elevator up to the eighth floor, where I pulled every book I could find on Michelangelo out of the stacks and spread them across one of the reading tables. Some of what I read in the books I already knew. Most of the information was new to me.

The same refrains and questions were raised repeatedly by many of the authors. How do we explain the very existence of someone like Michelangelo? How did he acquire artistic skills that seemed otherworldly when compared to the artists who preceded and followed him? And the all-important questions, where did he come from and how do we account for such a man?

The answers to those questions, I quickly learned, did not involve a family that was artistically endowed. Quite to the contrary, there was nothing about Michelangelo's family that was extraordinary. His mother and father were fairly ordinary people. They had five boys, four of whom were quite ordinary. In no way did they live anything other than commonplace, even banal lives. Yet the fifth son, Michelangelo, was universally acknowledged, both in his own time and in the years that followed his death, to be the greatest artist the human race had ever produced.

How is that possible? How can someone who was so universally acknowledged as a genius come from such a background?

I had hoped to find something in my readings at the library that might give me just the smallest clue as to why A. C. used Michelangelo's name in the opening menu of his computer. I found

myself instead marveling at the trick of fate that somehow produced Michelangelo.

I was back to my earlier suspicions that the only connection
between A. C. and Michelangelo seemed to be that my employer
was trying to steal one of the great artist's drawings, and perhaps
some of the other Renaissance treasures on display at the museum
of art.

As I prepared to return the books to the stacks, I suddenly noticed a bearded man staring at me from the other end of the room.
He quickly disappeared behind a bookcase. Moments later, when I
looked up, he was once again staring in my direction. As I walked
over to where he was standing, he stepped behind the bookcase
again. When I approached that area and peered around the corner of the bookcase, he was no longer there. He had disappeared
completely.

*He looked an awful lot like Waldo, the man who killed his wife in
the church rectory!*

• • •

I didn't tell Ilsa what I thought I had seen in the library. I didn't
know what she would think. I also didn't know what to think. I
began to question my own perceptions of the people I encountered
almost from the very moment A. C. came into my life. So I thought
it would be better to keep it to myself.

*Are these fears turning into obsessions? Was it really Waldo, or
had my imagination been playing tricks on me again?*

After I dropped Ilsa off at Balboa Park, I made a decision I had
put off ever since I took a leave of absence and moved out of the
rectory. I decided to return to the church where I had served as a
priest for several years. I didn't know what I would do once I got
there. I only knew it was something I needed to do, even if I only
drove by and relived those memories.

I drove north on Interstate 5 until I passed through Del Mar. A
few miles later, I turned east and drove into the community where
I had served as a priest. I passed several blocks of affluent homes,
most of which had spacious lawns and expensive ornamental land-
scaping. I did not notice a single *For Sale* sign, and there were
no foreclosed signs on the lawns of any of the large, multistoried
homes. The wealthy neighborhoods were a far cry from the Downtown area where I lived in my studio apartment.

I had grown accustomed to the poverty, the homeless people digging through dumpsters, the handwritten signs held by worn and tired street people, some with shabbily dressed children standing by their sides. I had never been aware of that side of humanity until I left the rectory. Now, as I drove through one block of beautifully landscaped homes after another, I realized the area where I had once served as a priest was not the norm. It was the exception. The great masses of humanity struggling merely to survive on the Downtown streets and alleys, living without hope or a future of any kind—they were the norm.

As I approached the rectory and church, I felt my stomach tighten. All of the anxieties I had wrestled with as I held the Rubik's Cube in the darkness of my studio apartment rushed back at me as I pulled up to the curb across the street from the rectory. It had changed little in my absence. The two-storied building with the beige stucco exterior and white shutters looked very much the same as it did the day I left in a taxi and started my new life on the edge of Downtown San Diego.

It looks so innocent, so perfect. No one new to the parish would know what had happened there.

I thought about getting out of the van and walking up to the rectory, and perhaps even going inside the church. But I knew I was not ready for that. The memories were too raw, too painful in their enormity.

Maybe someday, but not now.

I pulled away from the curb and made a U-turn at the end of the block. As I passed the church and rectory on the way back, I saw a single light glowing in the upstairs bedroom window where I had once slept. I watched the light until it disappeared behind the tall branches of a huge palm tree on the front lawn.

• • •

Ilsa stepped out of her apartment as soon as she heard me unlocking my door.

"Are you okay?" she asked. "You looked depressed when you dropped me off at the park."

"It's been a pretty eventful day," I explained. "A lot of things happening."

"Want to talk about them?"

"Sure," I said, gesturing for her to come into my apartment.

"So," she said as soon as she sat down in my reading chair, "you told me you thought someone got into your apartment. Is that what made it such an eventful day?"

"That's only part of it. I drove over to my old parish. I decided to revisit some old memories, even if they weren't the best memories."

"How did it go?" she asked sympathetically.

"I didn't stay very long. I just pulled up to the curb, thought about maybe getting out to see if the church was still open. But decided not to. Then I drove away."

"Something must have motivated you to go back."

"I didn't say anything to you on the way over to the library," I explained. "I didn't want to distract you from what you needed to do there. But the reason Tindal brought me down to police headquarters today was because another person I had contact with died."

"Another one?" she exclaimed, her eyes growing wide. "Who was it?"

"Two days ago, I drove over to St. Joseph's Church to be alone and think. A homeless man came in shortly after I did. He sat down in a front pew. When I left, he wasn't there anymore. I thought he had slumped down in the pew and fallen asleep. Tindal said they found him later in an alley."

"How did he die?"

"Tindal didn't say. I don't know what that means. Maybe he doesn't know yet." I quickly reconsidered my earlier decision not to tell Ilsa what I had seen in the Downtown library. I decided she needed to know. "Then, just this afternoon when you and I were in the library, I thought I saw the man who shot his wife in the rectory when I was counseling her. He was standing next to some bookcases. When I went over there, he stepped behind those bookcases and disappeared."

"Are you sure it was him?"

"No. I'm not. But from a distance it sure looked like him."

"What would he be doing there?"

"I have no idea. The worst-case scenario is that he was stalking me."

"Why?"

"I don't know."

"Are you going to tell the police you saw him?"

"No."

"Why?"

"It might not even be him."

"And if it was him?"

"Then there might be something to what Tindal has been saying all along?"

"What has he been saying?"

"He said I seem to be a lightning rod for a lot of very unusual things that are happening in this city."

• • •

While I waited for A. C. to return, I tried to get back into my daily running schedule. I needed something, anything to drive the gnawing obsessions out of my mind, if only for a few precious moments.

Early one Sunday morning, I drove over to Balboa Park and left the van on the western side of the Laurel Street Bridge. It had rained the night before, and I stepped into a small puddle of water as soon as I exited from the van. In the distance, on the other end of Balboa Park, a small rainbow arched across the sky and disappeared into a cloud layer in the east. Because of the early morning rain, the park was almost devoid of people. There were only two elderly women who were walking their small dogs on the grass near the Moreton Bay fig tree where I had spotted the transient sitting on one of the roots weeks earlier.

I started a slow, casual jog across the bridge and ran underneath the archway near the Museum of Man. That section of the park was also unusually quiet and devoid of people. I ran past the Old Globe Theatre, the House of Hospitality, the Timken Gallery, and the Museum of San Diego History. As I exited the park on the eastern end, I turned north on Park Boulevard and jogged for another two miles before turning around and starting back. Once I was back in the park, I decided to walk until I reached the Museum of Man, and then jog across the bridge back to my car.

I was approaching the Spanish-style buildings near the House of Hospitality, when I looked to my left and saw a man who was partially concealed behind one of the concrete pillars. His body was hidden, but I could see just enough of his head to know that I had seen him before.

Waldo! It's definitely him!

"What are you doing out here?" I yelled. "What do you want from me?"

Hearing my voice, he quickly retreated behind the concrete pillar.

My anger at what he had done the day he shot his wife in the church rectory overcame any fear I might have had regarding his reasons for being there. I quickly ran over to the concrete pillar to confront him. But when I approached the pillar, he was no longer there. I glanced in all directions and caught a quick glimpse of him disappearing behind one of the buildings farther west.

Any remaining fear of what he might do to me if I caught up with him vanished. I quickly ran in that direction, determined to catch him and find out what exactly had happened that day in the church rectory and why, apparently, he was stalking me. As I approached the Alcazar Garden, he again disappeared. I saw some movement behind one of the huge bushes on the southern end of the garden, and I sprinted in that direction.

He was not there either. Once again, he had eluded me.

I ran back out to the main street that ran through the center of the park to see if he had somehow made it over there without me seeing him.

Again, there was no sign of him.

It has to be him! I can't be imagining all of these things, can I?

• • •

I was determined to get some answers to why I was being stalked. Although a few days earlier, when I visited my old parish, I had decided not to enter either the rectory or church, I was now determined to go back and try to get inside. I needed to know if there was something I had overlooked the day Waldo shot his wife. Something that might explain why he was stalking me.

Did he also intend to kill me that day? If so, why did he change his mind after he shot his wife?

I drove north on Interstate 5 and took a series of side streets until I approached the church and rectory. I figured, since it was Sunday morning, the priest who now lived in the rectory would be busy with Mass. The secretary who worked in the rectory generally did not work on the weekends. So I was hoping I could get inside and just try to relive the horrible events that had occurred there several months earlier.

I heard the muffled sounds of voices in the church as I walked up to the rectory. I knew the front door would probably be locked, and it was. But I also knew the back door was seldom locked, even during Mass. I walked quickly around to the back of the rectory. As

I turned the knob on the back door and pushed gently so as not to make too much noise, it swung slowly open in front of me. I paused for a few moments and listened to see if I could hear anyone inside the rectory.

I could hear no one.

As I studied the interior, I created a cover story in my mind in case someone should find me back in the rectory without notifying anyone that I was planning to make a brief visit. I decided I would say that I had forgotten something in my old office, and I was returning to see if it was still there. I didn't know if that explanation would be convincing, but at least it was better than telling them my real reasons for returning to a place that held so many terrible memories.

I walked slowly down the hallway to the office, pausing occasionally and listening to any sounds that might indicate that someone was in the rectory. I could only hear the muffled sounds of the Mass that was being conducted in the church a short distance away.

As I stepped into the office, I saw that the new priest had made some minor changes in the arrangement of the furniture. There were also a few new books scattered across the desk and new carpeting. Still, the office looked very much the way it did the day I witnessed the murder of the unfortunate woman who came to me seeking advice on how to deal with her violent, abusive husband.

I studied the interior of the office for a few seconds and then sat down in the chair behind the desk. The memories of that horrible day quickly flooded over me. Nothing in those memories had changed. Nothing in them revealed anything new. Nothing, that is, except for one very small detail I remembered just before the police escorted me out of the room. Something that didn't quite match my memories of those few seconds as I walked past the dead body of the woman lying on the floor of the rectory.

As they led me out of my office, I glanced down at the lifeless body of the woman. One of her arms was stretched across the floor, her palm open and blood-smeared. A small hole in her hand indicated that the bullet had passed through her palm before entering her head. Her other hand was still thrust deeply into her purse, as though she was trying to extract another tissue to wipe her eyes.

The thing I didn't remember from my earlier recollections of those events was that the hand she had held up in the air was already holding a tissue. She had dropped it the moment she held her hand up to protect herself from the anticipated gunshot. The tissue was lying on the floor, only a few inches away from the hand with the bullet hole in the very center of the palm.

Why was she reaching for a second tissue when she already had one in her other hand?

• • •

How do you get inside the mind of a killer? And what do you do if you find something in there that's even more frightening than anything you could ever have imagined in your darkest, most unnerving speculations about the horrible things human beings can do to one another?

Those questions—and others—haunted me as I drove back to my apartment.

Why did the woman's husband continue to stalk me after he passed on the perfect opportunity to kill me in the rectory? In his deranged state of mind, did he suspect that I was involved with his wife? Was that it? Did he realize the absurdity of that moments after he shot his wife and became fixated on my collar? He had the perfect opportunity to kill me and eliminate the only eyewitness to the murder. Yet, he passed on that opportunity. Maybe later he had second thoughts and started stalking me, probably determined to finish what he had left undone in the rectory.

I suppose I should have expected that Detective Tindal would show up as soon as I returned to my apartment. It seemed that he always made an appearance whenever I changed my routine or did something even a little out of the ordinary. This time was no different. His car was parked outside my apartment building when I arrived. He stepped out of it and walked over to me as soon as I exited from the van.

"I take it you've been following me again," I said as I leaned against the driver's door of the van.

"I wasn't," he said, "but others have been keeping an eye on you."

"Why?"

"Well, let's just say for a man who claims he wants desperately to get away from something terrible he once witnessed, you certainly seem to go out of your way to go back to the place where it happened."

"I take it you followed me to the rectory?"

"Of course."

"Like the murderer always returns to the scene of the crime?" I asked. "Is that what this is all about?"

"Maybe."

"Is there another reason?" I asked.

"Look," he said, "just tell me why you went back. That's all I need to know."

"I was wondering if there was something I didn't remember clearly, something that might explain why all of this was happening to me. So I went back to my old office to see if it might trigger memories of something I had overlooked, something that . . ."

"Did it help?"

"Not really," I admitted. "But there was another reason I went back."

"And what was that?"

"Twice over the past few days, I thought I saw the man who shot his wife right in front of me. The man she called 'Waldo.' I thought I saw him in the Downtown library. And again in the park, just this morning."

"Is that why you were running around over there, looking behind every bush and concrete pillar, searching for something like a man possessed?"

"So you were there, too?"

"No, but there were others who said you were running around like a man who had taken leave of his senses and was chasing something only he could see. They wondered if maybe what you've been seeing is not what the rest of us have been seeing, including the way that woman was killed in your office."

CHAPTER SEVEN

My life as a priest had not prepared me for the maze I had stumbled into. I was not, by any stretch of the imagination, "street smart." I knew a little about running a small business, which was what I had to do as a parish priest. Except for an occasional funeral, I knew nothing about a world in which life and death seemed to hang in the balance each and every day, as was the case with many of the street people I encountered after I moved out of the rectory.

I was handicapped in another way as well. I was accustomed to searching for answers to my life's problems in books on philosophy and theology, the Bible—and especially prayer. But prayer no longer worked for me, and I could think of nothing I had ever read that cast any light on my current dilemma.

I was a babe in the woods, unable to navigate my way through the maze with the only tools I had acquired as a parish priest. I had been trained to search for answers and meanings through the religious symbols that surrounded me. However, those symbols usually had one fixed meaning that did not change over time. They were comforting and reassuring because they were always the same. The symbols I encountered in my new life, if they were indeed symbols, were constantly changing. Their meanings were always in flux and always demanded new attempts to reexamine and reinterpret them.

A. C. was at the center of that new world where nothing seemed permanent and everything was subject to reinterpretation. He was the great unsolved symbol upon which all the lesser symbols derived their meanings.

• • •

Three more days passed, and A. C. had still not returned. My mysterious employer was becoming even more mysterious in his absence. As the days passed, I continued to worry about my role in whatever plan he was putting together, but I was more concerned about what I had experienced in the Downtown library and Balboa Park. I even began to question my own state of mind.

Was it, indeed, Waldo I had seen, or was my mind playing tricks on me? Was I hallucinating? Had I imagined other things that happened after I witnessed him murder his wife in the church rectory?

In spite of what was happening to me, even if it was completely beyond my control, I continued to try to find a connective pattern that made any sense. This time, however, I did not look for it on my Rubik's Cube. I looked for it in the pencil drawing A. C. had made of the homeless people by the East Side Rescue Mission. I studied it for hours, marveling at its craftsmanship, while I asked myself one simple question.

What was his motive in making this drawing?

It wasn't merely the result of some absentminded doodling to kill time. It was too well crafted. Besides, A. C. had asked me to take him to that area with some purpose in mind—perhaps even to draw the homeless people.

Or maybe to recruit them for something else EWE International is planning?

I decided to look up an old acquaintance to help me understand what might have motivated A. C. to draw a picture so exquisitely detailed that the homeless people in it appeared to be looking out from another world that existed in a different dimension of time and space.

· · ·

When I pulled into the East Side Rescue Mission parking lot, it was teeming with activity. Volunteers and mission employees were busily sorting through huge boxes of clothing, trying to separate the usable items from the ones that had to be thrown into a huge rag bin. Two half-empty trucks of donated furniture were parked near a ramp. The truck drivers and their youthful assistants carried tables, chairs, and other items up the ramp and into the back of the mission. An ancient, rusty school bus was parked along one side of the building. As I walked across the parking lot, I passed some withered, flowerless jasmine bushes on opposite sides of the front door.

No one was sitting behind a small desk in the reception area, so I followed some handwritten signs that directed me down a long hallway. As I passed a huge, open doorway, I could see some of the city's homeless sitting in the cafeteria, eating at banquet tables spaced around a large room. The sounds of clanging pots and pans also echoed out of that area. Ahead of me, at the end of the hallway, I could see some sleeping cots and beds spaced around another large room. I turned left and entered a room that had a handwritten note taped next to the door that indicated it was "Father Timothy's Office."

I had phoned Father Timothy, the director of the East Side Rescue Mission, from a bus depot pay phone earlier that day to tell him I would be coming over. He was waiting for me in his office, which appeared to double as another storage area for donated items. Boxes of clothing were stacked along two walls, and a small cot was positioned in one corner. A coffee-stained, deeply scarred oak table, piled high with invoices and other paperwork, was located in the rear of the room.

Father Timothy was sitting in a badly worn desk chair behind the table, studying some of the documents. He hadn't changed that much since I last saw him. He was still the same elderly, chain-smoking priest with patches of snow-white hair on both sides of his head. In spite of his advanced years, he was robust and muscular. On the surface, he always appeared to be gruff and emotionally distant, but his eyes created the impression that he was deeply saddened by the human wreckage that existed just outside the walls of the rescue mission he had founded and managed.

"So you've been in hiding?" he said, looking up at me.

"I've been accused of that," I replied.

"*Are* you in hiding?"

"I guess so."

"So am I," he said.

"You? In hiding?"

"I might as well be. I never get out of here." He raised his right arm and gestured at the contents of the room. "I even sleep here. . . . So, tell me, have you officially resigned from the priesthood?"

"No. I'm on leave until I decide what to do next."

"When I was a parish priest," he said, "I often wondered if I was accomplishing anything with my life. I felt like all I did was dress up to look important. Over here we at least try to do some good, although I don't know that we save very many of the people who come to us for help. Their problems and addictions run pretty deep. Probably as deep as mine."

As he spoke, he reached for a cigarette stub smoldering on a nearby ashtray that was piled high with filters and ashes from previously smoked cigarettes.

"At least you found your true calling," I said. "I haven't come close to finding that insight into myself."

"One of the things I've learned," he said thoughtfully, "is that often what people think is their true calling, really isn't their true calling. It's only one small step on a much longer journey. I didn't fit in as a parish priest. Over here, in all this clutter and human wreckage, I fit in. What comes next for me is anyone's guess. You might find something similar happening to you someday, whether it be as a priest or something else you can't yet foresee."

I glanced at a framed photograph on his desk of a group of soldiers who were serving in the Vietnam War. The area behind them was deeply scarred with craters and defoliated trees. A single helicopter was rising in the air directly behind where they were standing.

Father Timothy saw that my gaze had shifted to the photograph. "Yes, that's me when I was much younger," he said, pointing at one of the men. "I was a chaplain over there. . . . Many of the homeless who come here for help are veterans of that war and other wars. But you probably know that."

As he studied the photograph, he lit another cigarette, inhaled deeply, and placed it in the ashtray.

"Recently, some homeless people in San Diego were murdered or died from unknown causes," I said. "Have you heard about them?"

"Only when I read the newspapers, which isn't very often."

"Have any of the homeless who come to this mission talked to you about it?"

"I've heard some talk. Not much. You have to understand that for the people who come here, life is one long, daily struggle with death. So they don't look at it the way the rest of us do. For them, people die on the streets all the time. Some are killed. Some die from natural causes. They don't talk too much about it. To them, it just happens. They try to protect themselves by sleeping in groups. But that's about all they can do."

"Did they know any of those who were killed?"

"I've never heard them mention anyone by name. Why do you ask?"

"Because I've had contact with some of the victims," I explained.

"In what way?"

"Just fleeting, brush-by contact. It was enough for the police to consider me a suspect."

"In the killings?" he asked.

"Yes."

"That's ridiculous," he said, gesturing toward the back alley that was visible through a dirt-streaked window in the rear of the room. "There are sick, twisted people out there. They see the homeless as less worthy to live on this planet. They're most likely the ones who are responsible for those attacks."

"I was witness to one killing in the church rectory," I said. "I'm sure you remember that. And then I had some coincidental contact with others who died under suspicious circumstances. I guess that's enough for the police to consider me a suspect."

"It's still ridiculous," he huffed. "You're not a killer. You've had a string of bad luck, but you're no killer."

"I'm glad you think that," I said. I pulled A. C.'s drawing out of my pocket and placed it on the table in front of him. "I've been driving a van for an elderly businessman who is confined to a wheelchair. He goes by the initials A. C. He claims he's an accountant for some big firm by the name of EWE International. I suspect he might be involved in something else, probably something criminal. Maybe something that involves the homeless. He drew this when I drove him over to this area the first day I worked for him. Do you recognize any of the people in this drawing?"

He studied the drawing carefully. "Yes, I recognize one of them."

"Which one?"

"The tall fellow in the back with the long hair. He comes over here sometimes to help us with the heavy lifting. We feed him and give him a little pocket money. I haven't seen him in a while though."

"What do you know about him?"

"Not much. His name is Joe Wolff. Some people call him Big Joe. He's part Native American. He's a Gulf War veteran. He's been struggling with post-traumatic stress disorder. He'll hang around here for a while, and then he'll suddenly disappear for days or weeks at a time. I think he can only take so many interactions with people, and then he has to be alone."

"Sometimes I feel like I'm struggling with those same symptoms," I admitted.

"You might be. It's more common than people realize. Any severe trauma can bring it on."

"Where might I find this Joe Wolff?"

"If he's not around here, he's probably Downtown in Horton Plaza. He likes it down there."

"Think he'll talk to me?"

"He might if you tell him I sent you over. What do you need from him?"

"I want to ask him why my employer made that drawing."

"Why didn't he just take a picture? Most cell phones have cameras."

"He doesn't have a cell phone."

"A businessman without a cell phone? In this day and age, that doesn't seem possible. Even we have cell phones, and we're hardly a Fortune Five Hundred company. How does he communicate with his business associates?"

"I don't know," I admitted. "I'm guessing they don't want anyone tapping into their lines and overhearing what they're planning. So he must have some other way of communicating with them. I've driven him to a number of business meetings that were obviously preplanned. But I don't know how they organized them."

• • •

After I left the rescue mission, I drove the van Downtown to the Horton Plaza area and parked in the basement floor of a multilevel parking structure. My footsteps echoed off the concrete walls as I made my way over to the elevator and up to the ground level. After I stepped into daylight and started walking toward Horton Plaza, I passed several huge corporate office buildings that surrounded a grassy area where many homeless men and women were congregating. I surveyed the area and spotted a large man with long hair sitting alone on a concrete bench. A. C. had captured him so perfectly that it looked like he had just stepped out of the drawing and sat down on the bench.

As I walked over to where he was sitting, I passed two homeless men who were engaged in various obsessive rituals with their hair and fingers. A woman who also appeared to be mentally ill put a protective arm around a plastic bag containing her life's possessions, apparently to guard them from anyone who came too close to where she was sitting.

"Joe Wolff?" I asked, walking over to the tall man sitting on the bench.

He cast a menacing gesture in my direction. Then he looked away as though he did not want to be disturbed.

"Father Timothy sent me over. He said you might be able to help me." I pulled the pencil drawing out of my pocket and held it out to him. "He identified you as one of the men in this drawing. I was wondering if the man in the wheelchair explained to you why he drew this."

"No, he didn't." Joe replied tersely as he glanced at the drawing and then continued to look into the distance.

"It looks like he had all of you pose for this drawing. Did he pay you to do that?"

"No."

"What—"

"He said he would feed us."

"He paid you with food?"

"Yes."

"I asked Father Timothy if anyone who comes to the rescue mission knew the homeless people who were killed in this area or talked about them. He said if anyone knew them, it would be you."

"I only knew one person who talked about those killings. He's also in that drawing."

"Which one?" I asked, holding out the drawing again.

"This one here," he said, pointing at a small, thin man with bushy hair and a small scar on his chin.

"What did you know about him?"

"I didn't really know him. Sometimes I would see him around the mission. I haven't seen him since we were all in this drawing."

"Do you know what happened to him?"

"No. He's probably camped out someplace else in this city."

"Did anyone around here ever wonder," I asked, "who might be behind the attacks on the homeless people in this area?"

"No. Those things happen when you live on the streets. Most of them never get into the newspapers. Why do you ask?"

"Because some people think the man who drew this picture was involved in those killings."

"I don't think so," Joe replied, shaking his head gently.

"Why?"

"He seemed like he was a businessman, but he wasn't like so many of the people who work out of those buildings," he said, gesturing at the corporate office buildings that towered above Horton

Plaza. "They ignore us. He didn't. I don't think he would have done something like that."

"Who do you think might have killed them?" I asked.

"I don't know. There was something different about that old man in the wheelchair, but I don't think he would kill anyone."

"Different? In what way?"

"He was just different. He seemed to understand us. . . . Listen, if you're looking for an enemy, start with the buildings that surround this park. That's where you'll find the real criminals. Not an old man sitting in a wheelchair drawing pictures."

• • •

Before going back to my apartment, I decided to stop for a glass of wine at Jake's Club while I pondered the significance, if any, of my conversation with Joe Wolff. I was staring at my image in the mirror on the back wall, just above the liquor bottles, when I felt a presence next to me. Tindal's face and upper body suddenly appeared in the mirror as he sat down on a stool. Sid immediately walked over, and Tindal ordered a tap beer.

"Thought you were going to report back to me about your employer's activities," he said after Sid placed the glass of beer in front of him.

"There's nothing to report," I replied. "He's still out of town."

"Have any idea where he went?"

"Nope. He never told me a thing about what he planned to do. . . . I did get into his apartment, though."

"What'd you find?"

"Nothing."

"Nothing?"

"No food, no clothes, no dishes or pots and pans. Nothing except the furniture the apartment came with."

"Sounds like the apartment across the hall from you," he speculated.

"Yup."

I debated whether to tell him about the computer in A. C.'s apartment, but decided against it. I was concerned that Tindal or one of his officers might try to confiscate it. I wanted more time for Ilsa and me to try to crack the code and reveal whatever secrets it might contain.

"What the hell do they do?" he asked. "Sleep in their apartments and slip out the door the next morning?"

"I'm not sure they do that much."

"Why?"

"There were no sheets or blankets either. Just one pillow."

Tindal was becoming more agitated and frustrated. "Who are these people?" he asked.

"Still think it's a drug cartel hiding behind fake addresses to conceal their criminal activities?"

"Maybe," he replied. "We're pursuing one lead that appears to be promising."

"Mind if I ask what it is?"

"He might be the accountant that he says he is. We've learned of an accountant who cooked the books for some shady international businesses. He fits the description, but his background is so murky it's been hard to come up with anything really concrete about him."

"Do you have any idea how he ended up in a wheelchair, or what he's doing out here?"

"If he is that accountant, he was playing with a rough crowd. There are rumors that he betrayed them. If so, he's lucky he got away with a couple of broken legs. They could have tossed him out of an airplane."

"How convinced are you that it's him?"

"The profile fits. The international companies this accountant worked for would move into an area and recruit the poorest of the poor to do their dirty work for them. Peddle their drugs, settle scores, things like that, while they maintained a veneer of corporate respectability."

"Sounds a lot like A. C.," I admitted.

"Yes, it does," Tindal said as he tossed down the last of his beer and stood to leave. "When he gets back, let me know what he's up to. I don't intend to let him play those same games in my town."

"Tell me something," I said. "Did one of your people get into my apartment the other day?"

"No, of course not," he replied, looking genuinely surprised. "Why do you ask?"

"Because my things were moved around when I returned to my apartment after I met with you Downtown. Looked like someone had gone through it searching for something."

"Wasn't us," he insisted.

Tindal quickly slipped out the door, leaving me alone to stare at my image in the mirror while I pondered the identity of my mysterious employer. Just that afternoon I had spoken to a homeless man who seemed to sense something good and decent in A. C. A few hours later, a detective who had seen the worst in human nature told me he suspected A. C. was just another criminal who had cooked the books for some of the most depraved and decadent international businesses on the planet.

Which one is he?

• • •

My conversation with Tindal made me even more suspicious of A. C. If he was the same accountant Tindal had described, then he was probably capable of almost any kind of deception. Before going back to my apartment, I decided to play a hunch and revisit the Mission Beach Pier where I had dropped him off the day he left town. The pier had seemed like a very strange place for A. C. to meet with his associates. It seemed more likely that they had rented one of the cottages on the pier, and they were using it as a meeting place.

Perhaps they are using it to finalize their plans to steal some of the priceless treasures from the art museum, or maybe to establish their contacts for future drug dealings in the area.

I decided to see if I could spot any of A. C.'s associates in or near one of the cottages. I weaved my way through Mission Beach's narrow streets and found a parking place not too far from the pier. As I approached the pier, I saw a small structure that was apparently used to register guests for the cottages. When I entered the office, a middle-aged man with sun-bleached, blond hair and darkly tanned skin was working behind the registration desk.

"I wonder if you could help me," I said.

"I can certainly try," he replied.

"Do you happen to know if a company by the name of EWE International has rented any of these cottages over the past few weeks?"

"I can't give out that information," he said. "But I can tell you that I've never heard of a company by the name of . . . How do you spell it?"

"Ewe, like a female sheep."

"Nope. I've never heard of a company by that name."

"How about *any* business renting those cottages recently?"

"No. Sorry."

Realizing any attempt to pry information out of him was use-less, I thanked him and walked out of the office. I decided to walk the length of the pier, while I looked into the windows and doorways of the cottages to see if the people A. C. had met with earlier were in any of them. I walked casually down the pier, pretending I was out for an early evening stroll. I didn't see anyone in the cottages other than families preparing supper or scantily clad young men and women preparing for a night of partying. The sun was setting on the western horizon, and the lights attached to the guardrails were starting to blink on as I passed the last cottage.

As I was about to leave, I noticed something in the distance. Everyone else, including the fishermen and sightseers, had left the pier for the night, but there appeared to be one lone figure sitting on a chair next to the guardrail at the very end of the pier. As I walked in that direction, I could hear the ocean surf slapping against the concrete pilings. When I reached the end of the pier, I recognized a familiar figure gazing out at the gathering darkness above the Pacific Ocean.

A. C. was sitting in his wheelchair in almost the precise spot where I had left him several weeks earlier.

CHAPTER EIGHT

"What are you doing out here?" I asked. "You said you were on a business trip."

"I *was* on a business trip," he said without looking up at me. "I got back today. I decided to spend my last night in one of those lovely cottages. I wanted to hear the sound of the ocean while I fell asleep. Where I come from, there is no ocean—or at least we have to travel a long way to get to one."

"Where *do* you come from?"

"Oh, I don't think it's necessary for us to talk about that. At least not now."

"I've been thinking about giving you back the keys to the van," I said. "I'm feeling uncomfortable, not knowing what kind of business you're in."

"I wouldn't want you to do that, Justin," he said, looking up at me and smiling warmly. "Everything will be clear to you in time."

"It's been very difficult—"

"Is it possible that we might be able to talk about this tomorrow?" he asked. "I need to take a trip to the Huntington Library to look over some business opportunities. We can talk on our way up there. I'll be waiting for you on the street by the registration office. Would that be okay with you? I'll pay you overtime."

"Yes . . . I just . . ."

"It's not often that I get to enjoy the sound of the ocean," he said softly as he stared again at the darkness gathering on the western horizon. "I would like to savor it for one whole night."

• • •

Before falling asleep that night, I made another visit to A. C.'s apartment on the third floor. Once again, I tried many different ways to break the Michelangelo code he, or someone else, had built into what looked like an otherwise conventional computer. Nothing worked. I finally gave up, removed the piece of paper I had stuffed into his door lock, and went back to my apartment on the first floor.

In the morning, A. C. was waiting for me on the street by the Mission Beach Pier. I helped him into the van, and we drove over to Interstate 5 and headed north. He was silent until we drove through Oceanside and entered Camp Pendleton.

"I know what you're probably thinking," he said finally.

I glanced in the rearview mirror and saw that he was staring out the window at the ocean side of the Marine Corps base.

"I wasn't thinking anything," I said.

"You asked last night what kind of business I was in. You're probably thinking the work of an accountant is incredibly boring and uncreative."

"No, I wasn't thinking that."

"What if I told you I have a very large clientele, and they expect me to do enormously creative things with their investments? Things that have considerable impact on this country and, indeed, the entire world."

"I would say that sounds like someone who is involved in the stock market."

"Yes, it does, doesn't it," he agreed. "But I can only make recommendations based on the accounts I keep for those I represent. That's why I'm technically an accountant, although my responsibilities extend beyond that narrow definition."

I wasn't sure how to respond to his comments, so I decided to ask him something else that had been on my mind.

"I found a drawing you made of the homeless people by the East Side Rescue Mission. It was in the back of the van. You obviously have artistic abilities."

"I left it there for you," he said matter-of-factly.

"Left it for me? Why?"

"I though you should see what many others see every day of their lives."

"Poverty?"

"Very few people see it, even if it is right in front of their eyes."

"You mean the very poor?"

"Yes, and other things as well."

"Is that why you drew the picture? Did you think I hadn't seen those people before?"

"Assigning motives is more difficult than most people realize," he replied. "Often there are several motives behind a single action.

It takes time to see how they all interact with one another. . . . I
have work to do now. We can continue our discussion on the way
back from the Huntington."

For several minutes, I concentrated on the scenery on both
sides of Interstate 5. When I finally looked into the rearview mirror
again, A. C.'s eyes were closed. He looked like he was either asleep
or deeply lost in some form of meditation.

• • •

A. C. did not open his eyes until we drove into the Huntington parking lot. To save on the wheelchair battery, he asked me to push him
over to the Huntington Art Gallery. As we moved slowly down one
of the narrow, asphalt-covered pathways, we passed several white-
stone statutes. They all looked like the same Greek or Roman god
in slightly different poses.

"Do you know who that is?" A. C. asked as we approached yet
another version of the same statute.

"It's one of the mythological gods," I said. "But I'm not sure
which one."

"It's Mars, the Roman God of War," he explained. "Just think,
in the middle of all these great art treasures, the planners of the
Huntington placed a small army dedicated to the god of war."

"Maybe they were placed there to protect the art works," I
speculated.

"Or maybe it was the other way around," he countered. "Maybe
art protects the world from war. Have you ever thought of that
possibility?"

Our conversation ended as soon as we entered the front door of
the Huntington Art Gallery.

"Meet me here in three hours," he said. "I have much to get done
today, but that should give me enough time."

As A. C.'s wheelchair disappeared down one of the long hallways and into an adjacent room, I took stock of what I might do for
the next three hours. A woman standing just inside the front door
was handing out brochures, and I asked her if I might have one. I
studied the index of the exhibits in the art gallery and decided to
explore the Renaissance wing on the second floor.

At the top of the staircase, I encountered a series of paintings
of various aristocrats from the fifteenth and sixteenth centuries.
The people in the portraits all wore lavish, expensive clothing, and

many had long strings of jewelry wrapped around their necks, apparently to remind anyone passing by that they were members of the wealthy ruling elite. One middle-aged man was bedecked in a wrap-around, fur stole, and he had several long strings of pearls draped around his neck.

I gradually wandered past the Renaissance portraits and made my way over to the wing reserved for biblical subjects. The walls of that room were covered with large fifteenth and sixteenth century paintings of the Madonna and child in various poses. Other paintings depicted the lifeless body of Christ draped across the laps of his followers after the crucifixion.

The painting that caught my attention was the smallest painting in the room. It measured no more than a foot long on all four sides, and it depicted the soon-to-be crucified Christ ascending Calvary. The description next to the painting indicated that it was the work of an anonymous Austrian artist who had painted it sometime between the years 1420 to 1440. The description also indicated that the title of the painting was *The Way to Calvary*.

The artist had captured Christ when he is surrounded by his tormentors who will soon crucify him. They appear to be angrily urging him to set a faster pace. The disciples and others follow closely behind, their heads down or tilted back in grief, knowing the horror that awaits them at the summit. In the rear of the painting, the tips of numerous spears are prominently visible against a pale-blue sky, a reminder of the military presence of the Romans in the Holy Land. The Roman guards themselves are concealed behind the people who follow Christ as they journey together up Calvary.

Only one figure in the painting seems ambivalent about whether he sympathizes with Christ, as do the disciples, or is annoyed with Christ for wasting their time by moving so slowly up to the summit, as do his tormentors. That figure is standing next to Christ and appears to be simultaneously urging him on, while holding up one arm as though to touch the cross and ease the weight from Christ's shoulders.

As I leaned closer to study the face of the bearded figure who was dressed in a blue robe and white cap, he reminded me of someone else. Someone I had seen in my grandmother's missal. It was filled with cards with religious and artistic depictions of biblical figures.

But that wasn't it. It was something else.

He looks like A. C.

• • •

Later that day I wandered into one of the many garden areas that were positioned like little islands across Huntington's spacious, park-like grounds. I found a concrete bench by some tall bushes and sat down while I decided how to spend the rest of my time before I had to pick up A. C.

As I gazed out over the flowing, green lawn and the many flower-covered bushes, I kept thinking about the painting by the anonymous Austrian artist. The resemblance between A. C. and the figure closest to Christ in the painting was uncanny. A modern artist could have superimposed A. C.'s head and face over the figure in the blue robe and white cap—and nothing would have been lost. It would still be the same painting, albeit A. C.'s captain's cap would have created somewhat of an anachronism.

As I pondered the latest mystery involving my eccentric employer, I kept thinking that he seemed to belong to another place and another time. Maybe, I speculated, the reason was because he really *did* belong to another place and another time.

Maybe he did step out of a Renaissance painting.

Suddenly, I heard voices in the garden area on the other side of the huge bushes behind where I was sitting. I turned and looked through some small openings in those bushes and saw what appeared to be the same group of men in business suits I had seen with A. C. at the convention center. A. C. was sitting in his wheelchair with his back turned toward me.

"Are we any closer?" I heard him say.

"We are getting very close," a different male voice replied.

"Do you think they will change their minds, or are they ready to go through with it?" another asked.

"I have tried to convince them what they must do," A. C. said. "However, we may be past that point. I will keep trying. But you must all be ready to do your part if—"

"If what?" someone asked.

"If it comes to that," A. C. replied.

As I tried to reposition myself to get a better view through a different opening in the bush, I heard what sounded like a collective sigh from the people gathered around A. C. Then I heard the sound of soft footsteps. When I repositioned myself again and

looked through the original opening in the bush, A. C. and his business associates had disappeared.

· · ·

Later, I met A. C. by the front door of the art gallery as we had
planned, and we started back toward the parking lot. Suddenly,
he held up his right hand and gestured for me to stop pushing the
wheelchair.

"There's one more thing I want to see before we leave," he said.
"There's a special exhibit on Archimedes in the Boone Gallery. Go
left up here and we'll take a quick tour of that exhibit before we
head back."

I pushed A. C.'s wheelchair over to yet another of Huntington's
many large, white-stone buildings. A banner strung across the
front wall of the Boone Gallery announced the special exhibit as
"The Secrets of Archimedes." Once we were inside the building, we
saw a large television monitor to our left. Two museum curators on
the television screen were discussing an ancient prayer book from
the tenth century that scholars had learned was created out of the
same parchments first used by Archimedes in the third century
BC. Using highly sensitive x-ray technology and other specialized
equipment, these scholars were able to see and eventually recon-
struct Archimedes's writings and diagrams. They were concealed
underneath the writings of the priest who cut up the parchment
into smaller pieces and wrote his prayer book over the top of Archimedes's original script.

A. C. watched the entire video, nodding occasionally and sometimes gently shaking his head in disapproval. When the video was
over, we slowly moved around the room, observing the other items
and reading the exhibit descriptions on the walls. One wall contained a long timeline that illustrated in considerable detail the
journey of the prayer book from when it was first written over the
top of Archimedes's manuscript in the tenth century, to when
scholars in 1999 started a project to read the erased text. The various displays described how scholars and scientists painstakingly
separated the pages and recovered the underlying letters and symbols that Archimedes had written.

The exhibit did not have the original prayer book, undoubtedly
because it was too valuable to risk putting on display. It did, however, have some facsimile pages of the prayer book with Archimedes's

writings highlighted in blue to make them more readable underneath the priest's writings. According to the exhibit descriptions, scientists concluded that Archimedes in the third century BC had developed mathematical theorems for the concept of infinity that predated by twenty-three centuries the mathematical breakthroughs that were needed to create the modern computer.

Before we left the special exhibit, A. C. paused to study a single frayed, stained, bacteria-ridden, smoke-charred page from the original prayer book that concealed Archimedes's revolutionary insights into the universe.

"They got most of it right," he said, "but not all of it."

• • •

For the first hour of our trip back to San Diego, A. C. studied some papers he pulled out of his briefcase. By the time we reached San Clemente, he seemed to have tired of his work and was instead staring absentmindedly out the window.

"Did you have time to tour the art gallery?" I asked, glancing into the rearview mirror.

"Not as much time as I would have liked," he said. "But I was able to visit it."

I decided to test his knowledge of the paintings I had just viewed and perhaps reveal more about himself.

"The collection of Renaissance paintings was very impressive," I said.

"Most people who view Renaissance paintings are so preoccupied with the biblical characters at the center of the paintings," he replied, "that they often fail to notice the figures on the peripheries. Are you aware of that?"

"What figures?" I asked.

"The angels. They are almost always there. Have you noticed them?"

"Sometimes."

"They are the angels who interact with human beings. Do you know who they are?"

"I know there are eight or nine different angels. I forget the order."

"The Seraphims are the closest to God," he explained. "The Archangels are much closer to the human race. They are a step above normal angels. In between are angels like the Warrior Angels.

They fight the evil spirits that attempt to dominate the universe. Surely you remember them from your Bible."

"I was aware of them, yes."

"Then you know that Archangels and other angels are often in those Renaissance paintings, hovering above or on the fringes, watching the suffering of those who are more human than they are. It's obvious the Renaissance artists believed in them."

"I saw one painting in the Renaissance wing that reminded me of you," I said.

"Which one?" he asked.

"It was a painting by an anonymous Austrian artist. It was titled *The Way to Calvary.* Are you familiar with it?"

"Yes. It is not a very famous painting. But I remember it."

"There is one person in the painting whose face looked very much like your face."

"Which person?"

"The one in a blue robe and white cap standing next to Christ," I explained. "He seems almost to be reaching for the cross, even as he is urging Christ along."

"I have a very generic face," he said. "Some have told me they have seen my face in paintings of *The Last Supper,* or standing at the cross during the crucifixion. Others insist they have seen my face in some of the paintings in your own museum of art. I think people see in a painting what they want to see. Why? I don't know. . . . I'm glad we did get over to the Archimedes exhibit, though. I enjoyed that very much."

"You seem to know a lot about Archimedes," I said.

"I've studied many of the great minds that have inhabited this planet. One can learn a lot from them."

"And what is their great secret?"

"They focus almost obsessively on their work, and they don't let anything distract them. Michelangelo was that way. So were Da Vinci and Sir Isaac Newton and Galileo and so many others."

"Certainly talent had something to do with it?"

"Of course, it did. But many people have had talent. . . . Let me give you an example. Do you know how Archimedes died?"

"No, I don't," I admitted.

"He was instrumental in creating military weaponry that helped the people of Syracuse survive a two-year onslaught by Roman soldiers who were determined to sack their city. One night, thinking the threat was finally over, the defenders of Syracuse lowered their guard, and the Roman soldiers breached one of the walls and entered the city. Archimedes was in his study at the time, unaware of what was happening. He was so involved with trying to solve a mathematical problem that had eluded him that when a Roman soldier came to arrest him, he refused to leave until he solved the problem. Angered by Archimedes's insolence, the soldier killed him. The real point to the story, however, is that even the threat of death could not divert Archimedes from solving the problem he had set out to solve. That's how focused he was."

"Think that characteristic is true for all artists and scientists?"

"Oh my, yes, especially for the great ones. The great scientists are that way. The great artists are that way. Sometimes a single person comes into this world with the ability to be both a great artist and a great scientist. Those are the ones who can propel the human race into a higher plateau of existence."

I pondered what A. C. had just told me. "I've always thought artists and scientists were on the opposite ends of the learning curve," I admitted.

"They don't have to be. The great creative forces that pulsate through the universe inform and guide both of them. They are like rare, beautiful, translucent fish swimming through a sea of sharks and other predators. They are unlikely to survive the journey, but when they do, they can create a better world." There was a long silence, and then he added, "And sometimes they make the world an even more difficult place in which to live."

• • •

Before he disappeared into our apartment building, A. C. told me he would not meet me again for two days. He said he needed time to get his thoughts together about the project he was developing. He did not stipulate what that project might be—only that it needed his undivided attention.

I decided to use the time to see if I could learn anything more about the painting titled The Way to Calvary I had seen in the Huntington Art Gallery. I was hoping the San Diego Library might have some books on the painting and where it originated. I was especially interested in learning whether there was ever any speculation about the figures in the painting, especially the man in the blue

robe and white cap. While I was at it, I thought I would also do
some research into the life of Archimedes, since A. C. seemed to
be especially knowledgeable about the great inventor and scientist.

I gathered several books from the stacks and retreated to the
eighth floor of the library, where I was surrounded by a tall, domed
ceiling with huge windows that allowed for me to look out over
the modern San Diego city skyline while I explored the ancient
past. None of the books had any information on the painting by
the anonymous Austrian artist. The title was not even included in
the indexes. I learned a few new details about Archimedes and his
contributions to modern weapons of war, but nothing significant
enough to give me any insights into why A. C. had found the Greek
scientist to be so intriguing. I don't know that I *did* expect to find
anything. I just thought I might stumble across some small needle
in that ancient haystack, even if it was covered over by layers and
layers of subsequent centuries.

After several hours of reading through the books, I finally gave
up. Before leaving, I decided to take the elevator up to the view
terrace that was located just above the eighth-floor reading room.
As the elevator door opened, I found myself looking out over a panoramic view to the west of Downtown San Diego. The Coronado
Bridge curved gracefully across the skyline, connecting San Diego
to Coronado Island. The tall, white pillars that supported the bridge
shimmered in the fading sunlight.

While I stood there, leaning on the guardrail, my thoughts shifted back to what I had learned about Archimedes. I realized that the
Coronado Bridge, which had been built in the latter decades of the
twentieth century, would probably never have been built had it not
been for the scientific and mathematical experiments he conducted
many centuries earlier. Nor could the towering Downtown library
building I was standing in have been built. In the distance, I could
also see the large naval destroyers and aircraft carriers that were
docked in San Diego's harbor. They, too, could never have been
built had it not been for Archimedes's experiments with buoyancy.
He was virtually the father of modern naval warfare.

*Without those breakthroughs, none of those things would have
been possible! Truly, Archimedes helped to build the modern world
and modern concepts of war!*

Suddenly, the elevator door behind me opened and Detective
Tindal stepped out and walked over to where I was standing.

"So did you learn anything new on your trip up north?" he asked.

"I take it you followed us up there?" I said.

"Of course, we followed you. What did you expect? Do you have any idea what was so important that your employer just had to visit the Huntington?"

"No, I don't," I admitted. "He met with some of the same business types he met at the convention center. That's all I know."

Tindal pulled a pack of cigarettes out of his shirt pocket, lit one with a small cylinder-shaped lighter, and inhaled deeply. As he exhaled, the smoke drifted leisurely into the panoramic scene in front of us and then quickly disappeared in the ocean breezes that swept gently out of the harbor.

"We're still following that lead I told you about earlier," he said.

"You mean the accountant who was involved with some shady international corporations?"

"Yes."

"Still think they did him in?"

"It's possible. It's also possible that they broke his legs to let him know they were serious. Maybe they wanted to teach him a lesson before they sent him out to recoup their losses by stealing art treasures or expanding their drug cartel into new areas. I don't know which one is more plausible. Probably both."

"If A. C.'s a common crook," I said, "he's a very well-educated one. He knows a great deal about world history and art history."

"He'd probably have to know a lot about art history if he was planning to steal some of it."

Tindal flicked the ash off the end of the cigarette and watched it fall over the guardrail toward the street below.

"His interests in art, science, and history seem very genuine," I said. "He's unlike anyone I've ever met before. He's very knowledgeable about everything."

"Don't get taken in too easily by him," Tindal countered as he flicked the cigarette stub over the guardrail. "That's what all con artists count on. They rely on people who trust that they are real and genuine. Once they accomplish that little sleight-of-hand trick, their victims are like putty in their hands. They can do anything they want with them."

"I'm sure you know them better than I do," I admitted.

"Stay in touch," he said as he turned and walked back to the elevator.

I stayed for a while longer as night settled over Downtown San Diego, the Coronado Bridge, and the San Diego Harbor. I was more confused than I had ever been before. I knew Tindal's warnings were based on his experiences with criminal types. Still, I struggled to place A. C. in that category. He seemed like something else, something far more complex.

• • •

My mind continued to wrestle with the Archimedes puzzle long after I had fallen asleep. In my dreams, I began to see the name Archimedes as though I were holding and reading the ancient parchment I had viewed in the Boone Gallery of the Huntington Library. Unlike that text, only two of the letters in Archimedes's name were highlighted in blue: the A and the C. The other letters in his name were less visible on the parchment.

A. C.!

In my dream, the letters slowly disassembled and were replaced by other letters that spelled the name Archangel. The same two letters were once again highlighted in blue.

A. C. again!

When I awoke later that night, I remembered the dream, and the questions about A. C. poured out of the depths of my subconscious mind like water pouring over the top of a swollen dam.

Is he a reincarnated Archimedes whose mathematical breakthroughs regarding infinity enabled him to master time travel? Did he return to undo the modern war machines he had done so much to create—or perhaps to make them even more powerful? Or is he an Archangel sent to change the course of human history—or maybe unleash some terrible vengeance on the human race? Or is he a corrupt businessman who is also a criminal mastermind? Or is he none, or all, of the above?

The multiple possibilities were tearing away at me. I wished to confine A. C. to a single, irrevocable identity, but every time I thought I understood him, or recognized him in a historical or biblical figure, some other part of him refused to complete the picture. He was like the Rubik's Cube I obsessively twisted and turned, trying get all of the colors to align on the appropriate sides. Yet, there were always one or two pieces that did not fit. Once again, I questioned my own state of mind.

Am I reading too much into everything? Isn't that an early sign of a nervous collapse?

Still, A. C. did not seem to be entirely of this world. He knew too much, and had experienced too many things, to be one person. He also refused to acknowledge where he came from. He seemed instead to be someone who had made his presence felt many times throughout human history.

CHAPTER NINE

was feeling more and more like I was surrounded by levitated pieces of some gigantic puzzle floating in the air, each piece searching for at least one companion piece with which it could interlock and create some small fragment of a much larger picture. Sometimes several pieces of the puzzle interlocked, but other pieces were left floating in the air, seemingly part of a different puzzle. Nothing I could do completed the picture.

I was also more than a little concerned about my own state of mind. My obsession was controlling my every thought. Some protective barrier had collapsed, and I was seeing A. C. as no one else was apparently seeing him. I tried to pull back from my obsession, and for a time I was able to do so. But the obsession always came back, each time more powerful than the time before.

Even in my more rational moments, I was convinced that A. C. was too knowledgeable about world history and art to be a common crook. He was more of a Renaissance man. He seemed to know a great deal about many different things. No one who was that well educated could be a common criminal.

Or could he?

Was it possible that he provided the perfect point man and cover for a drug cartel, as Tindal suspected? Posing as an international art dealer, he would have the perfect career to move into and out of many different countries without raising too many suspicions about his activities. Still, I was not at all convinced that Tindal had put his finger on A. C.'s true identity.

I decided to test one of the observations A. C. had made about himself. He said he was told that he resembled biblical figures in Renaissance and other paintings. He said some of those paintings were in the San Diego Museum of Art.

Was he deliberately trying to motivate me to look for his presence in those paintings?

As farfetched as that seemed, my obsession forced me to take another trip to the museum of art to see if what he said about

himself was true. I had never spent any time on the second floor of
the museum, so I decided to start there and work my way down to
the first floor.

On the way up the staircase, I noticed two huge oil paintings of
the Madonna and Child hanging on the walls. One of those paintings depicted the Madonna and a young baby Jesus. There were
no other biblical figures in that painting. The painting on the opposite wall, however, did have a figure that, with a little imagination,
might have passed for A. C. An elderly, gray-bearded, brown-eyed
man in a white robe and golden vestments was gazing at the Christ
child with awe and reverence. The painting was hanging too high
on the ceiling for me to get a closer look at any of the other details,
so when I reached the top of the staircase I walked into one of the
adjacent rooms.

I immediately encountered a painting titled *Saint Jerome* by
the Spanish artist Francisco de Zurbaran. Saint Jerome was also
depicted as a gray-bearded, brown-eyed, elderly man who wore a
circular-brimmed, red hat. He was pointing at a dove in the sky
while the vague image of an angry, menacing lion was snarling only
a few feet away from where he was standing.

Was this another one who looked like A. C.?

One of the most fascinating paintings I encountered on the second floor was Martin Bernat's *The Crucifixion*, which was painted
in the late fifteenth century. In this painting, the face of a gray-
bearded, brown-eyed, elderly man was only partially visible in a
small space between a Roman soldier on horseback and the thief
dying on the cross to Christ's left. No other part of the gray-bearded
figure's body was visible in the painting. He seemed out of place,
almost as though he was viewing the crucifixion through a different
set of emotions and from a greater distance than the others who
were gathered at Calvary.

*He looks like he doesn't belong there, as though he is an observer
who came from another time and place and has little in common with
the other figures in the painting.*

I knew I was allowing my imagination to run wild. Most likely, all
of the figures who bore even a faint resemblance to A. C. were stock
figures that painters at the time used to create elderly characters
who were needed to fill some gap in the canvas. However, there did
seem to be an unusually large number of paintings in the gallery
that contained at least one gray-bearded, brown-eyed, elderly man
who bore some resemblance to A. C. If nothing else, those figures

validated the imaginations of others who told A. C. he resembled figures they had seen in Renaissance paintings.

Or perhaps I am so desperate to understand who he might be that I am allowing myself to engage in speculation that would be quickly dismissed by anyone truly knowledgeable about those paintings.

As I wandered through the biblical exhibits on the second floor, I remembered my first reaction to A. C.'s request that I call him by his initials, and not by his first or last name. At the time, I assumed he meant for the initials to be an abbreviation for the "accountant" he claimed to be, although I didn't know why he preferred to be identified by his profession as opposed to his real name. As a former priest, however, when I heard the initials "A. C.," I immediately thought of something else.

Do those initials stand for "After Christ," translated from the Latin "AD," and not "Accountant"? Is he on a celestial mission to heal the damage that had been done on Calvary?

That, too, seemed wildly imaginative.

I had one other thought I decided to check out before I left the art museum. During my first visit to the museum, while I waited for A. C. to return from an adjacent room, I had noticed Albrecht Durer's woodcut of *The Four Horsemen of the Apocalypse* on one of the walls. I remembered thinking that there was something a little curious about that woodcut. I decided to take a closer look at it before leaving.

After I walked down the staircase and entered the exhibit room, I stood for some time in front of Durer's woodcut. I had studied the Book of Revelation in the seminary, and I remembered St. John's vision of an apocalypse that would destroy planet Earth and all who inhabited it. Still, I could only stare in awe at the Four Horsemen—Death, Famine, War, and Conquest—as they unleashed their apocalyptic attack on the human race. As I studied their faces, most of my attention was focused on one of the riders.

He resembles A. C. more than any of the figures in the paintings on the second floor.

• • •

Before leaving the museum, I purchased a postcard copy of Durer's woodcut of *The Four Horsemen of the Apocalypse*. Then I retreated to my apartment. Using the postcard as a starting point, I decided to revisit a book I hadn't read in a long time. My Bible had been gathering dust in my bookcase ever since I moved out of the rectory and into the studio apartment. Now I hoped the original descriptions of the horsemen in the Book of Revelation, together with the postcard, might help me establish a more detailed connection to A. C., if one existed.

I paged through the Bible until I found St. John's descriptions of the horsemen in Revelation 6: 1-8. The first horse was described as "a white horse, and its rider had a bow. He was given a crown, and he rode forth victorious to further his victories." I remembered from my theology classes that there was some controversy over who or what the rider on the white horse might symbolize. The professor told us that some scholars believed he represented Christ riding across the earth during the Second Coming to reclaim his kingdom from the powers of evil that had corrupted the human race. Other scholars believed the rider on the white horse symbolized the very antithesis of this view. They believed he was the Antichrist, and he had been unleashed to conquer the earth and all of its inhabitants. That revelation exposed a frightening possibility.

Could the initials A. C. stand for Antichrist or the followers of the Antichrist?

The second horse in the Bible was described as "a red one. Its rider was given power to take peace away from the earth, so that people would slaughter one another. And he was given a huge sword." In the Durer woodcut, the rider had his sword raised high in the air as he prepared to slaughter the people who had not yet been trampled by the horses. An angel, who appeared to be gently smiling in approval, hovered high above this rider with its left hand extended, almost touching the raised sword. The angel seemed to be depicted as an emissary from God who was bestowing a benediction on the carnage that was about to commence. Most scholars, as I remembered, believed this horse and rider symbolized the horrible wars that would precede the end of the world.

Does A. C. have something in common with a red horse that symbolized war?

The third horse in the Bible was described as "a black horse, and its rider held a scale in his hand." In the Durer woodcut, the rider on this horse was the largest figure in the apocalyptic scene, and he held a scale of the type used to weigh grain. His horse was also the largest and most powerful of all the horses in the woodcut. The message Durer seemed to be trying to convey was that Famine, as symbolized by the black horse and its rider, would consume all the food sources on planet Earth, leaving the human race to starve itself out of existence. The sheer size of this horse and rider suggested that Durer believed Famine was an even more efficient instrument of death than War, as symbolized by the red horse and rider.

Does this explain what is happening to the bees?

The fourth horse was described in the Bible as "a pale green horse. Its rider was named Death, and Hades accompanied him. They were given authority over a quarter of the earth, to kill with a sword, famine, and plague, and by means of the beasts of the earth." Durer seemed to understand the irony in this description of the fourth horse and rider because, although the Bible had indicated they "were given authority" over all other means of destroying the human race, he had depicted both horse and rider as the smallest, most emaciated figures in the entire scene. Yet, they were the most powerful because they controlled, or were the end result of all the other instruments of destruction.

So there they were, all four of them: Conquest, War, Famine, and Death. But what do any of them have to do with A. C., if anything?

The rider on the first horse, who symbolized either Christ or Antichrist, bore a resemblance to A. C., but the rider on the second horse, who symbolized War, looked like A. C. had posed for Durer while he was creating that character for his woodcut. The resemblances between A. C. and the other figures in the paintings I had viewed earlier could be dismissed as coincidental. It was more difficult to dismiss the rider on the red horse. The facial resemblance was too strong.

Then there are the other similarities as well. A. C. has his own red horse: a wheelchair with a reddish-burgundy leather seat and backrest. He also rests his feet in stirrups of sorts—the metal footrests on the wheelchair.

Once again, I began to question whether I was seeing connections where I should be seeing coincidences. Still, there was something in the face of the second rider in Durer's woodcut that would not allow me to accept the most logical conclusion to what I had just discovered. I sensed something else, something far more powerful and alarming.

Is A. C. one of the modern-day four horsemen? Are he and his associates involved in an effort to create a major world war and subsequent famine? Or are they working to create a famine first, followed by a world war as nations fight over the remaining food sources? With a little imagination, one could extract the letters A and

C from the word Apocalypse and have the abbreviation A. C. Is he the very symbol and organizer of a coming apocalypse?

It was too much to think about. Once again, I had overwhelmed myself with an endless string of speculations that most rational people would probably quickly dismiss as the idle ramblings of an unstable mind. Still, I could not let go of my speculations. They bred suspicions of the worst kind regarding A. C. and EWE International.

• • •

Later that day, I found Ilsa working behind the Organ Pavilion in Balboa Park. She was examining something in her open palm when I walked up to her.

"More dead bees?" I asked when I saw what she was holding.

"Yes," she nodded grimly.

"How bad is it?"

"Wherever I go now, they're spread all over the ground."

"I've been reading about the biblical plagues and famines," I said. "Think this could cause a famine in our own time?"

"Yes. I don't think most people understand how serious this is. A newsletter I get pointed out that one out of every three bites of food we eat is pollinated by honey bees. We're definitely heading for a worldwide food shortage if this continues."

"You told me earlier that there are those who believe someone is deliberately killing the bees to cause food shortages."

"Yes, I remember telling you that, but I don't believe it's true. . . . Why do you bring that up?"

"Because if someone wanted to destroy us, a deliberate famine would be the easiest way to fight a war, since no one would even know they're in a war until it was too late. Or, perhaps if whatever is killing the bees could be controlled, it would enable ruthless people to corner the food market and raise prices to exorbitant levels, thus starving entire nations. If their motive was to eliminate the problem of overpopulation, it would also accomplish that."

"But what could anyone possibly gain if the entire planet loses the ability to pollinate its plants and grow food?" she asked. "They, too, would die, along with the rest of the human race."

"Maybe what's killing them isn't a part of this planet."

"What do you mean by that?" she asked.

"Maybe someone or something has their eye on this planet and wants to get rid of us before taking it over."

"That sounds a little farfetched. It overlooks the most likely culprits."

"Which are?"

"Chemicals and pesticides."

"Yes, but do we know who's unleashing them?"

"They hide their tracks pretty well," she admitted. "But scientists are closing in on them."

"Have you ever read about the Four Horsemen of the Apocalypse in the Book of Revelation?"

"Yes, of course."

"One of the predictions, according to some scholars, is that a worldwide famine will trigger a global war that could end the human race as we know it. Or it could be the other way around. A world war could unleash weapons so powerful the planet would lose its ability to produce food. In either case, the human race could not survive such an apocalypse."

"I worry about that every day," she lamented. "But why have you been thinking about it?"

"I believe A. C. and the company he works for might be involved in the death of the bees. They might be trying to destabilize the planet through famine and war."

"Why?"

"I don't believe they're a human corporation. I think orders for their hostile takeover come from elsewhere. As crazy as it might seem, I think they're working for someone who wants to take over Earth and use it for their own purposes, whatever those might be. I don't know who they are or where they come from. But if they really want this planet, the easiest way to acquire it would be to kill the bees. Everything else in modern civilizations would soon collapse like a row of dominoes."

"You have some proof of this?" she asked.

"No."

"If you're really serious, why don't you go to the authorities with what you suspect?"

"Who would believe me? They would think I was stark raving mad, which I probably am."

"They would ask you the same questions I'm asking you," Ilsa said. "I'm a scientist. I need proof. They also need proof before they can act."

"I don't have any," I admitted. "But I strongly suspect we might be in the middle stages of a biblical prophecy."

"And you believe the man you call A. C. is part of this prophecy?"

"Tindal thinks he might be an accountant who embezzled money from some shady international corporations and is trying to repay them through various criminal activities. I don't think so. I think there's more to him than that. We might be witnessing an epic struggle that was prophesized by Saint John in the Book of Revelation thousands of years ago, and A. C. might be at the center of it."

"What if he's just a harmless, eccentric old man, and not the mastermind behind some worldwide conspiracy?"

"I suppose that's also a possibility," I admitted.

• • •

As I walked back to the van, Detective Tindal pulled into the parking lot. He drove up to me and rolled down his window.

"Learned something I thought I'd share with you," he said.

"What is it?" I replied.

"I think we've finally figured out who your employer is."

"What'd you find out?"

"Remember that accountant I told you about, the one who cooked the books for some shady international corporations?"

"Yes, I remember you telling me about him."

"Well, his name is Arnold Davis."

"What's significant about that?" I asked.

"His middle name is Clark. So his first and middle initials are A. C. It can't be a coincidence."

"No. It probably can't," I admitted. "Did any of your sources tell you what happened to him?"

"Only that the international corporations he worked for were a criminal conglomerate. They hired some hitmen to find and kill him. Or else they did find him, busted up his legs, and then sent him out to recoup their losses. He got mixed up with some of the most ruthless people on the planet. It might account for some of the strange murders that have been occurring here."

"In what way?"

"We've always had our share of street criminals. But our city has become a battleground for some powerful criminal organizations, possibly even terrorist organizations that want the same thing. They seem to be fighting each other the way the organized crime families fought one another back in the 1930s. Only these people are far more organized and stealthier. They contract out their dirty work, while they keep up the appearances of respectability."

"Are you going to arrest A. C.?"

"Not yet. He'd be out on bail in a couple of hours, and then he'd disappear, and we'd never find him." Tindal reached for a cellphone and charger cable on the passenger seat and handed them to me. "I know you have an aversion to phones," he said. "But I want you to keep this with you at all times. It's a simple flip-top phone. I wrote the number on the back of the case. Press and hold the number two at any time if you need me or have learned something I need to know. It's the speed dial to my cellphone. It also has a tracking system so we can keep an eye on your whereabouts at all times. If we can connect your employer to even one of those murders, we'll move in and arrest him."

"So you want me to try to find that connection?"

"Yes. But remember, everyone is probably expendable to the people he associates with. You'd be no different than any of the others they've already eliminated."

• • •

I stayed awake much of that night, once again pondering the identity of my mysterious employer. The possibilities now ranged all the way from harmless old man to criminal mastermind who had embezzled a fortune from some of the world's most ruthless international corporations.

In the light of what Tindal had told me about Arnold Clark Davis, my suspicions that A. C. might not even be of this world, but was instead part of a hostile takeover of Earth as predicted in the Book of Revelation, seemed even more wildly imaginative. It seemed impossible that A. C. could be anyone other than the accountant who had created so many powerful enemies for himself.

Why am I so willing to jump to the more bizarre conclusions about A. C.? Doesn't that say more about me than it does about him? What void am I trying to fill that needs an otherworldly explanation for his unexpected presence in my life?

CHAPTER TEN

probably would have unequivocally accepted Tindal's characterization of A. C. as an international criminal if A. C. hadn't made a rather unusual request of me the very next morning. It was not a request I would ever have expected to hear from an accountant who, according to Tindal, "cooked the books for an international criminal conglomerate."

"Take me to one of your churches," A. C. said as soon as he was seated in the van.

"Which one?" I asked.

"The one you attend."

"I don't attend church anymore."

"You haven't been in a church lately?" he asked.

"Only the one where I sometimes go to think," I explained.

"That one will do."

After we parked the car and entered St. Joseph's, A. C. paused halfway down the aisle to study the paintings of the biblical subjects on the walls.

"Looks like someone was trying to imitate Michelangelo," he said. "They did a pretty good job."

He pressed the switch on the wheelchair's armrest, and I walked behind him as we moved slowly down the aisle. As we passed the front pew, he stopped, sat silently, and gazed up at the white, marble statue of the crucified Christ high on the wall behind the altar.

"You may leave me here," he said moments later.

"Do you want me to wait in the back?" I asked.

"No. Just leave me here. You may do whatever it is you want to do with your time today."

"When should I pick you up?"

"At five. I will be waiting for you right here."

He dismissed me with a gentle wave of his hand, and his gaze fixed once again on the statue of the crucified Christ. He entered into one of those focused stares I had seen so often before when he decided to block out all distractions so he could concentrate on whatever was more important to him at the time.

As I drove away from the church, I continued to question A. C.'s motives. It wasn't like he had asked me to drop him off at some prearranged church where he could meet with his business associates. Apparently, no such meeting had been scheduled. Every indication was that he just wanted to spend the entire day sitting in his wheelchair in a church.

Where does Arnold Clark Davis fit into that scenario?

If Davis was the criminal mastermind Tindal described, he certainly didn't seem like the kind of person who would sit in a church all day for no apparent reason. Unless the people A. C. had met with before knew where he was and planned to meet with him later, it seemed like a very strange request.

How will they even know what church he's in?

I decided to see if I could find anything at all on Arnold Clark Davis. I drove over to the Downtown library and set up shop behind one of the computers. For several hours I searched the Internet for any kind of information on Davis. There was nothing. If he existed, he must have grown up in a vacuum and disappeared into a vacuum.

• • •

Later that morning I decided to drive over to Balboa Park to see if Ilsa could take a break and join me for lunch. She agreed, and we settled into a small delicatessen near Fifth and Laurel. We sipped on iced tea while we waited for our lunch order.

"I met with Tindal after I talked to you yesterday," I said. "He intercepted me in the parking lot and gave me this."

I pulled the cellphone out of my pocket and placed it on the table.

"Why'd he want you to have a cellphone?" she asked.

"So I could call him in an emergency. It also has a tracking device. I think that's the real reason he gave it to me."

"So he knows we're sitting here having lunch together?" she speculated.

"Probably."

"Did he have anything new to tell you?"

"He said they've learned the identity of the accountant who embezzled money from some shady international corporations and then disappeared."

"Who is he?" she asked.

"His name is Arnold Davis."

"Think he's A. C.?"

"Are you ready for this?" I asked.

"Probably not. But tell me anyway."

"His middle name is Clark. Arnold Clark Davis."

"Those are the same initials. It has to be him."

"Most likely."

"How can you say 'most likely'? How many accountants are there with the initials A. C. who have that kind of background?"

"Not many, I'm sure."

"Where is he now?"

"In church."

"Church?"

"He asked me to drop him off at a church," I explained. "Any church. So I drove him over to St. Joseph's on Beech Street. He's going to spend the day there."

"Doing what?"

"I don't know. When I left, he was sitting down front in his wheelchair staring at the statue of the crucified Christ hanging on the wall behind the altar."

"That doesn't sound like something a criminal mastermind would do," Ilsa speculated. "He must have some other reason for being there."

"I know. It sounds more like something a harmless, lonely old man would do. Just to be alone in a church with his thoughts."

"But it must be him," she insisted. "It can't be coincidence that he has the same initials as the accountant who disappeared."

"You're right," I agreed. "It's probably him. But why would someone with that kind of criminal background want to sit in a church all day?"

• • •

My curiosity about A. C.'s reasons for spending an entire day in a church was so strong that I decided to drive back to St. Joseph's after lunch, slip inside, and see if anyone had joined him there. One of the front doors was open, so I slipped into the foyer and walked quietly down a side aisle until I approached the front of the church. I concealed myself behind one of the large concrete pillars and peered around the corner.

A. C. was still sitting where I had left him. I could only see the back of his head. So I didn't know if he had fallen asleep, or if he was still staring at the statue of the crucified Christ. In either case, he hadn't moved the wheelchair one inch since I left him there earlier that morning.

• • •

Later that day I found a parking place near Horton Plaza and walked over to the grassy area where many of San Diego's homeless congregated. I spotted Joe Wolff sitting on the same bench where we had talked during my first visit. Whereas most of the other people in the park huddled together in small groups, he was again alone.

"Joe," I said, walking over to him, "I'm Justin Moore, one of Father Timothy's friends. Do you remember me?"

"Yes," he said, nodding. "I remember you."

"I've been asked to check into the background of the man who drew the picture of you and the other men near the East Side Rescue Mission."

"Who asked you to do that?"

"The police," I admitted.

"What do they want with him?"

I sensed that I needed to be completely straightforward with him, or he would retreat back into his self-imposed shell and say nothing more.

"They still think he might be involved in some criminal activities."

"The police think that about everyone except those who live in the wealthier parts of this city."

"Is there anything you haven't told me about him that I should know?" I asked. "It's important to me. I need to know who I'm working for."

"He's not a criminal," Joe replied emphatically.

"Why are you so sure of that?" I insisted.

"Do you know how he fed us after he drew that picture?"

"I guess I just figured he took you to a fast food place."

"No. It wasn't like that at all."

"So how did he feed you?"

"He kept pulling sandwiches out of those two pouches on the sides of his wheelchair."

I was surprised by his explanation.

"He had sandwiches with him?" I asked.

"Yes, he did."

"I'm surprised they didn't spoil. I drove him around to many different places that day before I dropped him off at the rescue mission."

"They were as fresh as though someone baked them in the back room of one of those buildings and brought them out to the street to feed us."

"Maybe," I speculated, "those pouches were lined like the insulated cooler bags people take with them to the supermarket."

"Maybe," he nodded. "But I doubt it. Do you know how many people he fed out of those leather pouches?"

"I suppose the people who were in that picture he drew."

"That's how it started. But a crowd soon gathered around that wheelchair. He kept pulling sandwiches out of those leather pouches until everyone had one."

"How many people do you think were there?"

"Probably forty or fifty."

"Those pouches aren't big enough to hold that many sandwiches."

"I know . . . listen," he said, pointing at the tall buildings that surrounded Horton Plaza. "Like I told you last time we met, if the police are looking for enemies, they shouldn't be looking for them down here. They should be looking up there. That's where the real enemies are."

• • •

As I drove out of the Downtown area, I pondered how A. C. could possibly have made or purchased that many sandwiches. He didn't have any food in his kitchen, and there wasn't a store or bakery anywhere close to the apartment where we lived.

Is it possible he had them delivered to his apartment? But even if he managed to purchase the sandwiches, he would never have been able to stuff them into those pouches. They are made for a few miscellaneous odds and ends, not something that bulky.

I suddenly spotted a familiar figure sitting on a park bench near Third Avenue. He was dressed better than I remembered. But it was clearly Philip Walker, the homeless man who had organized the memorial service for Ruth Morgan.

"Phillip," I yelled as I pulled up to the bus stop and rolled down the passenger window.

He leaned slightly forward, a puzzled look on his face, and tried to peer into the side window of the van.

"It's me, Justin Moore," I said, "one of Ruth Morgan's friends."

The name Ruth Morgan seemed to jar his memories, and he stood and walked over to the passenger window.

"How's your family doing?" I asked.

"Much better, thank you," he replied.

"What are you doing down here?"

"I had a job interview. I'm waiting to catch a bus back home."

"Jump in," I said. "I'll drive you there."

"That's mighty kind of you," he said as he opened the passenger door and climbed into the van. "Every bus token I can save helps."

"Still occupying the same house?" I asked as I pulled away from the curb.

"You haven't heard?"

"Heard what?"

"Someone bought that house and several other foreclosed houses in that area."

"So where are you living now?"

"The same house. Whoever bought them is allowing the homeless like my family to live there rent free, so long as we keep the place up. They're even paying for the utilities."

"Who bought them?" I asked.

"We don't know. But with my wife and children having a place to live, without the fear of being evicted at any time, I've been able to look for work again."

"Did you sign a renter's agreement to stay in that house?"

"Nope. No one did. Not in our house and not in the other houses that were purchased and opened up to homeless families."

"So you know nothing about whoever it was who bought those homes?"

"All I know is that I looked out the window one day," Phillip explained, "and saw a man in a very expensive business suit pull the foreclosed sign out of the yard and throw it in the back of a white van. I thought he was probably there to evict us. Instead, he came to the door and said we were free to live there as long as we wanted. Then he got into the van and drove away. I talked to some of the other homeless people I knew who had occupied other foreclosed homes. They had similar experiences."

"What did he look like?"

"Like any other businessman who works out of those corporate buildings Downtown. He didn't show any emotion or give any reason whatsoever for why he was doing this. He said the company he works for had purchased the property, and we were free to live there as long as we wanted so long as we kept it up."

"Someone's name must be on the deeds."

"I went down to the San Diego County Recorder's Office and tried to find out who owned the property," Phillip explained. "They pointed at a row of public computers and told me I needed to do my own research. However, the deed must have been filed under an unknown, perhaps fictional name. I could not navigate my way through the maze. On the way out, one woman who worked there whispered that I should check with Father Timothy at the East Side Rescue Mission. She said he might know more about the real owners."

• • •

Father Timothy was sitting behind his desk, sorting through a mountain of paperwork, when I walked into his office. He looked up and smiled as I entered.

"You're back," he said. "Come here to volunteer?"

"Not yet," I replied. "Maybe someday, but not yet."

"So what is it this time? Did you ever talk to Joe Wolff?"

"Yes, I did."

"Was he able to help you answer the questions you had about that drawing you showed me?"

"Yes. But that's not why I came by today. I just learned that you might be involved in the purchase of some homes near the Downtown area. Apparently, they were opened up to the homeless families who have been struggling to survive over there."

"Well, I guess you could say I'm involved. But I know very little about what happened."

"How's that?"

"I received a fax from some unknown donor who wished to remain anonymous. He said he wanted to purchase several foreclosed homes for the East Side Rescue Mission and open them up to the homeless families. I said, yes, of course, we would be interested in anything that would provide shelter for those people. I didn't think anything would come of it. Couple of weeks later, I received a letter

from the County Recorder's Office telling me I owned those properties with the stipulation that they be used only to provide housing
for the homeless."

"You know nothing more about the person who bought them in
your name?"

"Nothing. I'm not even sure what to do with them, other than
to let those families live there. It sounds like all the utilities will be
paid, upkeep and maintenance taken care of, insurance and taxes
paid. Other than that, it's as much of a mystery to me as it is to the
people who live in those houses."

While I considered what Father Timothy had just told me, I surveyed the contents of the cluttered room. As much as I lived on the
edge of poverty in my studio apartment, he had outdone me. The
only recognizable personal item in the room was his cot, and even
that looked like it had been handed down through several generations of previous owners. There was no clothes closet, no sink, no
adjacent toilet, no wall hangings—nothing that suggested personal
ownership of anything except the one framed photograph of Father
Timothy standing in the middle of a group of soldiers during the
Vietnam War.

"What's it like living here?" I asked.

"Probably different than anything any parish priest has ever
experienced," he replied.

"Do you even have time to be a priest?"

"I'm often on my knees, sorting through piles of clothes. That's
when I pray. It takes my mind off the arthritis in my shoulders and
hips and makes the time go faster. Everything I do over here that's
priestly is usually combined with something that needs to be done
to keep this place running. . . . Why do you ask?"

"I was just wondering," I said evasively.

"There must be some reason you asked," he insisted.

"I guess I'm still trying to figure out what to do with my own
life."

"I was only half kidding when I asked you to come over here
to volunteer. You should spend a few days with us. See what the
people who come to us really have to do to survive. It might help
you make your decision."

"Think it would improve my state of mind?"

"I don't know if it would improve it. It would certainly help clarify
some of the things that are troubling you. Over here, I go through
every emotion known to the human race in a single day. Hope,

despair, a sense of futility, occasional glimpses of optimism—it's all here. Each and every day. This is no permanent sanctuary for anyone. We don't have the resources. But every so often we see what we do really change a life and pull someone permanently off the streets. We live for those moments. They keep us going and bring us renewed hope."

"I think I might also have experienced something recently that gave me renewed hope."

"What was that?" he asked.

"Remember the man who hired me to drive his van? The one who goes by the initials A. C. Joe Wolff told me something quite amazing about him."

"What'd Joe say?"

"He said after A. C. drew the picture I shared with you, he pulled some sandwiches out of the leather pouches on his wheelchair and handed them out to the homeless who'd gathered around him."

"What's amazing about that?"

"Joe said he handed out forty or fifty sandwiches to the homeless," I explained. "Those pouches aren't big enough to hold even half that many sandwiches."

"That sounds like something Christ did with the miracle of the loaves."

"Yes, I know."

Father Timothy seemed genuinely puzzled by what I had just told him. "Where is your employer now?" he asked.

"He wanted me to take him to a church. Any church. So I took him to Saint Joseph's. He said he was going to stay there all day."

"Doing what?"

"Staring at the statue of the crucified Christ."

"That's it?"

"I checked on him a couple of hours ago. He's still sitting in his wheelchair where I left him, still staring at that statue."

"Has he told you yet who he is?"

"No. He hasn't. But I think he might be the one who bought those homes and deeded them to you for the homeless."

• • •

As I drove out of the rescue mission parking lot, I had the strong sense that Father Timothy was suppressing a deep concern for my mental health and stability. He seemed to listen attentively to the stories I told him about my mysterious employer. But I sensed something else in Father Timothy's countenance. He didn't say it as much in words, but there was a subtle expression of concern, maybe even doubt, that what I was telling him about A. C. might be the product of an overactive imagination, maybe even mental instability.

I decided to return to the church earlier than A. C. had requested. I wanted to see if anything unusual was happening. I slipped into a pew near the concrete pillar where I had watched him earlier that day. If he was aware of my presence, he did not acknowledge it. He continued to sit motionlessly in his wheelchair, gazing upwards at the statue of the crucified Christ.

The only change was that he had taken off his captain's cap. It was the first time I had seen him without his cap, and he looked older. He was completely bald on top of his head, and some dark-skin blotches and scars intermingled with the wrinkled, white skin of his scalp. Without his cap, he looked like someone who had aged a great deal during the time he had sat in his wheelchair at the front of the church. While I watched him, I found myself asking the same question I had asked myself so many times before.

Who is he?

I had avoided one other possibility, mostly because it seemed too farfetched to consider. But after what Joe Wolff had told me about A. C.'s ability to feed so many of the homeless with sandwiches he pulled out of the leather pouches on his wheelchair, I began to wonder if the more farfetched possibility deserved a closer look. With his cap off and his face silhouetted by the fading sunlight in the church, A. C. no longer looked so much like the rider on the red horse in Durer's woodcut.

He looks more like the rider on the white horse! The one some scholars think is Christ returning to vanquish the evil forces that hold the human race in bondage, while other scholars are equally convinced it is the Antichrist coming to conquer all of Earth and its inhabitants.

• • •

As soon as A. C. and I were back in the van, I demanded answers to some of the questions I had been asking myself for weeks, but never had the courage to ask him.

"Who are you?" I demanded to know.

"Why is that so important to you?" he replied calmly.

"Because I need to know who I'm working for. Those people you've been meeting with. Who are they?"

"They mean you no harm."

"What kind of business are you really in?" I insisted. "Are you working for some philanthropist who is trying to feed and house the homeless people in this area? Or are you releasing something toxic that is destroying the bees? Are people next? Is that it? The van's registration papers say you work for EWE International. What are they creating here?"

"You will know in time," he replied evasively.

"I need to know now."

"I have bought us some time. A few more days. Not any more than that. I have one final chance to change everything. After that, I will not be able to do any more."

"Why do you need me for whatever it is you're planning?" I insisted.

"You're more important than you realize," he explained gently. "The day will come when you will know that, although you might not recognize it at the time."

"The only thing I've accomplished is to see a lot of people die unnecessarily."

"If we don't change what is coming," he insisted, "there will be many more people who die."

"Just give me one solid reason why I should trust you!" I demanded.

"It has always been like this. You and others like you always believe you stand on the precipice. On one side, there is light. On the other, darkness. You do not understand that sometimes the darkness overwhelms the light. This could be one of those times if things do not change."

"That's not good enough," I demanded. "I need something real. Something I can feel, hear, touch. . . . Tell me just one thing. Is your real name Arnold Clark Davis?"

"Why do you ask?"

"He embezzled money from some international corporations. Some people think you're him."

"Who told you this?"

"A San Diego detective."

"Is that why you're carrying a cellphone now?"

"Yes."

He looked out the window as though contemplating what he wanted to say next.

"I've been many people, and I've been in many places," he said softly. "I carry them all inside of me."

"Does that include the place you were today?"

"In the church?"

"Were you reliving something you experienced before?"

"He suffered terribly."

"You were at Calvary when Christ was crucified? Is that what you're trying to tell me?"

"It's always the same enemies," he mused quietly. "Different faces, but the same enemies."

"There's a woodcut by Albrecht Durer called *The Four Horsemen of the Apocalypse.* Have you ever seen it?"

"Yes, of course I've seen it."

"It depicts Conquest, Famine, War, and Death as the four agents that could end life on this planet. Are you and the company you work for plotting a similar kind of apocalypse by wiping out the bee population to create a worldwide famine?"

"You have it backwards."

"What do you mean?"

"We're trying to save the bees, not kill them."

• • •

I don't remember anything more about our trip back to the apartment. I must have been lost in my thoughts. I don't remember dropping off A. C. I don't remember locking the van and walking inside my apartment. When I was next aware of my surroundings, I was sitting in the darkness of my apartment, having apparently just awakened from a deep sleep. My thoughts slowly focused on the events from earlier that day in the church and East Side Rescue Mission. I remembered the many references Father Timothy had made to the *New Testament,* even though that meeting—like the events in the church and the van afterwards—also seemed vague and distant.

I decided to turn on the light by my reading chair and retrieve the Bible from my bookcase. I returned to my reading chair and paged through the Bible as I refreshed my memories regarding what Father Timothy had referred to as the "miracle of the loaves." I felt like I was reading those passages in the *New Testament* for the first time, not attached to the demands of a sermon for Sunday Holy Mass or for classroom visits at the parish school.

All four of the disciples—Mathew, Mark, Luke, and John—described Christ's feeding of five thousand of his followers with five loaves of bread and two fish. Mathew described how Christ "broke the loaves, and gave them to the disciples, who in turn gave them to the crowds." Afterwards, when the remaining fragments of bread and fish were gathered up, they filled "twelve wicker baskets."

Mark, Luke, and John also described the incident in virtually identical terms, including the number of people who were fed, the five loads of bread, the two fish, and the twelve wicker baskets that were filled with the fragments afterwards. Mathew and Mark also described another time when Christ fed four thousand of his followers with seven loaves of bread and a few fish. These miracles of the loaves helped to set Christ on a collision course with the Roman authorities because it convinced his followers that he was truly a "king," albeit he rejected that title.

Is A. C. following in that tradition when he fed the homeless with the sandwiches he pulled out of his leather pouches? Is he somehow gifted with the same ability to multiply the loaves of bread until they can feed a huge crowd of people?

Joe Wolff estimated that A. C. fed some forty or fifty homeless with the sandwiches.

Does that parallel the five thousand people Christ fed with five loaves and the four thousand people he fed with seven loaves of bread?

Once again, I wondered if I was reading too much into an incident that might have a simpler explanation. I looked up from my Bible and stared at one of the long, discolored streaks that extended across virtually one entire wall of my studio apartment. As I stared at the brown streak that had been created by some earlier spill on the second floor, it occurred to me that I might have overlooked something important.

Christ had handed the loaves of bread to the disciples, who in turn parceled them out to the thousands of hungry followers.

I pulled the drawing out of my pocket that A. C. had made of the homeless before he fed them. I quickly counted them.

There are twelve!

CHAPTER ELEVEN

A. C. made another unusual request the next day. He asked me to drive him to the Fort Rosecrans National Cemetery in Point Loma, the same area Ilsa and I had visited on her research trip to check the bee populations. On the way out to the cemetery, he engaged me in another of those obtuse philosophical conversations that always left me searching for his intended meanings and intentions.

"How well do you know history, Justin?" he asked as we made our way through some heavy traffic in the city of Point Loma and then turned south on Catalina Boulevard.

"Probably a fair amount," I replied.

"How well do you understand the forces that *shape* history?" he asked.

"Probably the same answer."

"Most people think it's the big events that shape history. It's not. It's the smallest things imaginable. They are what shape history. A cough, a pause to study a flower, a step to the right instead of to the left—those are the things that shape history. After that, everything on the planet moves in a different direction than it might otherwise have travelled."

Minutes later we passed through the gates of the naval base and soon entered the military cemetery that was located on both sides of the peninsula that jutted south toward Mexico. A light fog hovered above the horizon on the Pacific Ocean side of the national cemetery. The San Diego Downtown skyline was visible in the east. On that side of the peninsula, several large military ships were docked in the harbor. Further south, other military and commercial ships were dry-docked and surrounded by huge cranes. Thousands of white, marble cemetery stones lined the sloping embankments on both sides of the narrow road that ran down the very center of the peninsula. The stones were lined up with the same kind of precision the military used in close-order marching drills.

When we were in the middle of the cemetery, A. C. said, "Turn left." Almost immediately, he said, "Stop right here."

I followed his instructions and parked next to a large tree that was surrounded on all sides by a sea of white, knee-high gravestones.

"Too many wars," A. C. said softly as he looked out the side window.

"Do you want to get out here?" I asked.

"Yes," he said. "I'll be spending the rest of the day in this cemetery. Come back at twilight to get me."

After I helped him get out of the van, he pressed the switch on the wheelchair armrest, and I watched the wheelchair move slowly toward a slight elevation in the middle of the sea of white stones. A. C. remained seated for a time. Then he used the wheelchair's armrests to push himself to his feet. He took a few awkward steps, paused, and stood motionless.

As he stood there, an ocean breeze began to blow across the cemetery, and the trees and grass arched gently in an easterly direction. Almost immediately, a light fog drifted in from the ocean, flowed over the top of the peninsula's summit, and shrouded the eastern side where A. C. was standing.

• • •

I heard a strange, pulsating noise as I was leaving the cemetery. I was so unaccustomed to the sound of a cellphone that at first I was not sure what to make of it. Then I remembered I had placed the phone in my front pocket that morning before I met A. C. in the foyer. I parked the car just outside the cemetery and flipped it open.

"Justin," the voice at the other end of the line said, "this is Bob Tindal."

"Yes," I replied.

"I thought it was time that one of us check in. I see you're in Point Loma this morning."

"A. C. wanted to see the military cemetery," I explained.

"Is he with you now?"

"No. He asked me to leave him there."

"Do you have anything new for me?"

"Nope. Nothing at all. He's just visiting various places in San Diego and asking me to pick him up later."

"Well, I have some more news about that accountant who disappeared."

"Arnold Clark Davis?" I asked.

"Yes, him. We have some reliable sources back east who knew we were looking for him. They said their own sources have told them he's dead. Apparently, the hitmen those international corporations hired might have caught up with him. Beat him up pretty badly and then threw him in the ocean several miles from shore. Sounds like whatever is left of him is probably in the belly of a shark."

"Then A. C. can't be him," I said.

"No. Unless he's an awfully good swimmer, he can't be Arnold Clark Davis. But we haven't been able to verify the story. That will take some time. There might be something else going on here, too."

"What's that?"

"It's possible your employer might be posing as Davis."

"Why would he want to steal the identity of a criminal who was beaten to death and thrown into the ocean?" I asked.

"Beats the hell out of me. But I've seen stranger things than that in my career."

"So what's your latest theory about this whole thing?"

"I'm guessing he must have known this Davis and decided to continue the business, whatever it might be, after he was killed and his body dumped in the ocean."

"Do you still suspect it's a drug cartel or international art thieves?"

"Maybe, although it's beginning to look more like a terrorist organization that's preparing to do some serious damage to this country. There's a huge military presence in this area. Lots of potential targets. That's another possibility we're looking into. The feds are starting to get involved. . . . Look, I'll be getting in touch with you again. I want to talk to a few more people back east. Then I think we'll have you bring your boss in for a little talk. Maybe he can enlighten us on what he's up to. We may need to take him into custody."

I sat in my car for several minutes after we finished the telephone call. I was not sure how much Tindal knew about A. C.'s background. Nor was I sure what Tindal's motives were for wanting me to bring A. C. in for questioning. They had him under surveillance. They could take him into custody at any time. They didn't need for me to be involved.

Maybe Tindal is testing me to see how deeply involved I am in whatever A. C. is planning? Or maybe they just want to keep following us around until A. C. reveals EWE International's real identity and plans for this area.

Then another thought, one even more ominous, occurred to me.

This is beginning to seem like some kind of ancient allegory scripted to be played out in modern times. Am I being set up like a modern-day Judas to turn over to the authorities a perfectly innocent man who poses no harm to anyone? Is A. C. like one of the Christ figures in the Renaissance paintings of the crucifixion? Is he on a mission of peace—and I was ordained to play the role of the Great Betrayer?

• • •

Later that day I sat alone on a stool while Sid, the bartender at Jake's Club, talked to some regulars at the other end of the bar. They were swapping humorous stories and periodically leaning back on their stools and erupting into laughter. Above their heads, there was a soap commercial showing on the television mounted to the wall near the ceiling. Eventually, Sid broke away from the group and walked over to wash some glasses.

"Saw you in here the other day talking to that police detective," he said.

"How did you know he was a detective?" I asked.

"I've been bartending for almost thirty years. After a while, you kind of know when the police are around."

"Well, you're right. He's a detective."

"Do they know anything more about those murders in the park?"

"He didn't say."

"Remember when I told you about that strange fellow who came in here? The one who was killed in the park."

"Yes. I remember you talking about him. You said he acted like he had amnesia or something."

"Mac, one of my regulars, remembered him, too," Sid explained. "He brought it up last time he was here. It seemed to bother him quite a bit."

"How come?"

"He said he ran into that same fellow at The Huntress down the street. Mac doesn't say much, so when he does, you know it's about something that has affected him deeply."

"Do you know how I can get ahold of him? I'd like to ask him what happened."

"He's not hard to find," Sid explained. "He keeps a pretty regular schedule. You could almost set your watch by him. Every morning he starts out over here with a couple cups of coffee. Around eight in the morning, he switches to beer. He'll have two beers, three at the most. Then around ten, he'll walk over to The Huntress and sit there for another two or three hours, nursing a beer or two. After that, he'll walk Downtown, hitting the bars along the way. It's how he's been living his life for as long as I've known him."

"Where do you think he'd be now?"

"He's still at The Huntress," Sid said, glancing at his wrist watch. "He'll be there for probably another thirty to forty-five minutes. Then he'll head Downtown. . . . One bit of advice, though. Like I said, he's normally a pretty quiet fellow. But if he starts talking about baseball, he's got these stories that are awfully hard to believe."

"Why's that?"

"He's got this story about how he could once hit a curveball. But some strange characters came into his dreams and told him they had other plans for him. Said they didn't want him in the major leagues. So they did something to his eyes that made it impossible for him to pick up the spin on a curveball. He still blames them for destroying his baseball career."

• • •

The Huntress was a small bar located on the corner of Laurel and Fifth, very close to the Laurel Street entrance to Balboa Park. I had jogged past it many times but had never gone inside. On the outside, it looked like a relic from another era, surrounded as it was by newly constructed, high-rise office buildings and condominiums.

Sid had told me I wouldn't have any problem recognizing Mac because he would be the only person at The Huntress who was wearing a New York Yankees baseball cap. When I entered the bar, I heard the clicking of pool balls in an adjacent room. Mac was sitting alone at the very end of a bar that was shaped like an elongated hockey stick.

"Are you Mac?" I asked, walking up to him.

"Ya," he replied tersely.

"Bartender at Jake's said I might find you here."

"What's he want?"

"Nothing. I'm the one who needs something from you. I live across the hallway from one of the men who was killed in Balboa Park. Sid said you knew something about him."

"Are you a cop?" he asked suspiciously.

"No. I'm just trying to find out what happened to my former neighbor."

"You sure you're not a cop?"

"No. I'm not a cop."

"I don't really have a lot to tell you," he said. "I was only around him for a very short time."

"Sid told me you heard him say something that bothered you a great deal. Could you tell me what he said?"

"Well, he was just sitting here. Right at this bar. There was a stool between us. When I looked at him in the mirror, his eyes . . . they just weren't right."

"In what way?"

"He looked like he was here, but not really here. And he was kind of mumbling to himself. At first, I couldn't understand a thing he was saying. Then he blurted something out that really made me wonder who I was sitting next to."

"What did he say?"

"He mumbled something about being sent out here to kill someone. He repeated it a second time. Then he looked in my direction. He must have thought I had overheard him because he gave me a real dirty look. I pretended I didn't hear what he had said and just kept looking in the mirror like I was lost in my thoughts."

"Did he say anything else?"

"Nope. Couple of minutes later he just up and walked out the door. He was a scary fellow, though. Something about him was real dangerous looking. And then, when I saw he had been killed in the park, I figured someone must have gotten to him first."

"Did you think about going to the police?"

"Nah. I didn't want to get mixed up in it. Besides, he's dead. He couldn't hurt anyone now."

"Sid told me you were a baseball player," I said.

"Yup."

"He said you almost made it to the major leagues."

"I *would* have made it to the major leagues except for one thing."

"What was that?"

"I could hit any kind of pitch, including a curveball, until one night I had a dream. The people in that dream told me I would no longer be able to pick up the spin on a curveball. They told me they had something more important for me to do. . . . What's more important than being able to hit a curve ball?"

"What did the people in your dream look like? Did you see their faces?"

"I don't remember their faces. I only remember they were wearing expensive-looking business suits. I have no idea how they got into that dream because I've never spent any time around people like that. Yet, it was almost like they were standing over my bed, looking down at me."

• • •

When I returned to the Fort Rosecrans National Cemetery later in the afternoon, I looked for A. C. in the area where I had left him, but he wasn't there. I drove the entire length of the peninsula, while I searched the harbor side of the cemetery for any sign of him. I circled the Cabrillo Monument at the very end of the peninsula and searched the ocean side of the cemetery on my way back. Occasionally, I got out of the van to walk down the western embankment to look for him. Finally, I saw him in the distance. He was in an area that did not seem like it would be accessible to a wheelchair, yet he had somehow maneuvered his way over there. He was staring at one of the knee-high, white cemetery stones as I approached.

"I looked for you on the other side of the cemetery," I explained. "That's why I'm late."

"Do you know who this is?" he asked, gesturing at the cemetery stone.

The name on the stone was "John Martin Whittier," and the dates of his birth and death were "March 18, 1944—August 7, 1971." The stone indicated that he had died in the Vietnam War.

"No," I said, "I didn't know him."

"I don't really know him either," A. C. said. "But I've been sitting here thinking about him. I've visited many of these graves today. You can still feel the sadness that surrounds all of them. You can feel the presence of those who gathered around these graves as someone played taps on a bugle, and they said good-bye to loved ones who died in foreign wars. Their collective grief is overwhelming."

"Is this grave any different than the others?" I asked.

"In some ways, yes. It's one of the saddest graves in this cemetery. You can still feel the sadness clinging to this very spot. There were people here who loved him very much."

I felt a cool breeze start to blow in from the ocean, and I watched as a naval destroyer cleared the harbor and moved slowly out into the open ocean. In the distance, the sun was starting a slow descent into the horizon.

"Are you ready to go back to the van?" I asked. "It's starting to get a little cold out here."

"In a moment," he replied.

"Were you ever in the military?" I asked.

"No. But I've been in many wars."

"How is that possible if you were never in the military?"

"My work kept me at a distance. But I saw the horrible atrocities that were committed in those wars. The broken bodies. The bloodied corpses. The shattered minds. The women and children weeping over graves. I saw too much of all that, and I felt like I should have done much more."

"In what way?"

"When you throw a stone into a pond, you never know where the final waves that flow from the center will end. Everything flows outwards. Everything affects everything else." He paused and appeared to be deeply lost in thought as he stared at the gravestone for John Martin Whittier. "Remember what I told you earlier today about the forces that shape history?"

"Yes, I remember you talking about that."

"If this young man had taken one step backwards, instead of one step forward," he said softly, "it would have changed the world."

As shadows crept across the white gravestones, A. C. slowly turned his wheelchair around and gazed out over the Pacific Ocean. In the distance, the naval destroyer I had seen earlier was disappearing on the horizon.

As I watched A. C. stare into the distance, I realized I had buried many parishioners and comforted their friends and loved ones, but I never allowed myself to feel their pain. Yet A. C. was sitting in an unfamiliar cemetery, surrounded by the gravestones of thousands of soldiers he had never known, and he seemed to feel the pain of each and every one of them.

The depth of his grief made me feel inadequate again. I had never truly shared the grief of my parishioners. I had only performed some rituals and said a few words over the graves of their loved ones. But I had never felt their pain. At least I had never felt it the way A. C. felt it as he somehow maneuvered his wheelchair down to the grave of a soldier who had died in the Vietnam War.

• • •

On the way back from Fort Rosecrans, we stopped at the intersection of First and Laurel to allow a group of disabled children in wheelchairs to cross the road under the supervision of their adult caretakers. From the way the children's heads slumped against their chests or shoulders, I knew it was the same group I had seen in Balboa Park.

"I saw them a few days ago in the park," I said as the wheelchairs rolled slowly across the street directly in front of us.

"I've seen them, too," A. C. replied.

"In the park?" I asked.

"No. I've seen them in many different places."

"As a former priest, I probably shouldn't say this," I admitted somewhat reluctantly, "but I struggle with trying to understand why they have to go through so much just to live."

"They will not be forgotten," A. C. replied.

When the last of the children had crossed the road, I glanced in the rearview mirror and saw A. C. watching them. A single tear had formed in the corner of his left eye. He closed his eyes briefly, blinked twice, and looked out the window once again at the wheelchairs disappearing around the corner of a house. He slowly raised his wrinkled hand to his face and wiped away the tear that had by then traveled almost to the corner of his mouth.

• • •

Ilsa stepped out of her apartment door as soon as she heard me turn the key in the lock of my own apartment. "Bought some Chinese food," she said, holding up a large paper bag. "There's enough for two, paper plates and all, in case you haven't eaten."

Once we were in my apartment, she sat down in my reading chair, and I positioned two pillows as a backrest and sat down on the bed. As I divided the Chinese food onto two paper plates, she glanced at the Rubik's Cube on the end table next to her.

"Still trying to solve that?" she asked.

"Not really," I said as I handed her one of the plates and leaned back on the two pillows. "I've been too busy trying to solve the other puzzles in my life."

"Still trying to figure out who you're working for?"

"That and a lot of other things."

"Such as?"

"I don't remember if I ever told you about Joe Wolff, the Native American who was in the drawing A. C. made of some homeless men. I've talked to him twice now. He thinks A. C. comes from some other world. I'm beginning to think he might have a point. . . . Joe said he saw A. C. feed forty or fifty homeless people after he finished the drawing."

"Why does that make him otherworldly?"

"He pulled those sandwiches out of the leather pouches on his wheelchair. There's no way he could have stuffed that many sandwiches into those pouches. They're not big enough."

"Maybe they go deeper than you think."

"Not that deep. Then I just learned that someone bought up some older foreclosed homes and turned them over to homeless families. Whoever it was asked Father Timothy at the East Side Rescue Mission to front for him. Father Timothy has no idea who put up the money for those homes. I'm thinking it might be A. C. and the company he works for because the person who pulled the foreclosed sign out of one of the yards was dressed the way A. C.'s business associates dress."

"Shouldn't those transactions be in the public record?" Ilsa asked.

"They're concealed behind a maze of fictitious names," I explained. "But apparently the deeds are in Father Timothy's name."

"It sounds like the work of some eccentric philanthropist," Ilsa speculated. "Maybe that's who your employer really is. Maybe he's just a harmless, elderly gentleman who has lots of money. Before he dies, maybe he wants to give it away to people who have nothing."

"I suppose that's another possibility in a long list of possibilities," I agreed. "But Tindal thinks he's involved in something more nefarious."

"Like what?"

"There's a huge military presence here. Navy, Marines, Coast Guard. I think Tindal is concerned EWE International might be a terrorist group plotting something against the military. But I'm not sure he's on the right track."

"Why?"

"If it's a terrorist threat, I don't think it has anything to do with the military. I think it's something else. I think they're stealthier than Tindal and the feds give them credit for. I think they might be responsible for the huge bee die-off in this area."

"And you think A. C. is the mastermind behind this threat?" Ilsa asked.

"No. I think he might be in opposition to it, and he's trying to convince his superiors, whoever they might be, not to go ahead with whatever they're planning."

"I still think he's probably a harmless, eccentric philanthropist with a lot of money to give away," Ilsa insisted. "I think all of you are probably reading too much into him. Besides, he pays his bills and lets you use his van. That doesn't sound like someone who's a front for a terrorist organization."

I envied Ilsa's ability to dismiss any thoughts that could not be supported with scientific proof. She never allowed herself to get sidetracked by abstract speculation. I admired it, but I also knew I did not have the same gift. I was often hopelessly sidetracked by speculation when I needed to focus more on the facts.

"I hope you're right," I said. "By the way, remember the night you slept over here when you said you heard voices and thought someone was in your apartment? If it was a dream, did you get any sense of how that person was dressed?"

"I'm not even sure it was a dream. But no, I only heard what I thought were voices. I didn't see anything or anyone. Why do you ask?"

"I met someone today who had a dream that changed his life. It reminded me of your dream, except that he remembered how the people were dressed who were in it."

"What are you suggesting?"

"I really don't know," I admitted. "It just seemed a little strange. . . . But right now, everything seems a little strange."

CHAPTER TWELVE

The next morning when I met A. C. at the mailboxes, he seemed more tired than I had ever seen him before. Every movement, even the effort to raise his hand to press the switch on the wheelchair's armrest, seemed labored and exhausting. He looked like a man who had not slept in several days and desperately needed to spend the day in bed.

Once we were in the van, he asked me to drop him off at a house on the corner of Kalmia and First Avenue. As we approached that area, I saw an old, brown and white Victorian home on the corner. A huge porch with white guard rails seemed to circle the entire house. Some dead orange and lemon trees were in the front yard, along with other dead vegetation. The house looked like it had been restored and then allowed once again to weather unattended beneath the Southern California sun.

"Drop me off right here," A. C. said as we approached the house. "Pick me up at three this afternoon."

I parked by the curb and helped him out of the van. He pressed the switch on the armrest of the wheelchair, and I watched as it moved slowly up to the front porch. From there, the wheelchair turned onto a partially concealed concrete walkway, disappeared behind some tall bushes, and soon appeared again on the front porch. I heard A. C. rapping on the door, and a woman in a long dress opened it. She was partially concealed by shadows from the interior of the house as she opened the door wider. As soon as A. C. entered the house, she shut the door behind them.

My telephone started to ring even as the door was closing behind A. C.

"Justin?" Tindal said.

"Yes."

"Remember yesterday when I said we'd probably be bringing your employer in for some questioning."

"I remember that, yes."

"Well, that's what we're going to have to do. We've learned a lot more about Arnold Clark Davis. Your employer could be Davis. And if he's not, he could be an imposter picking up where Davis left off."

"Where did he leave off?" I asked.

"Davis was deeply involved in several terrorist organizations. So anyone associated with him is up to his eyeballs in terrorist activities. We need to find out what your employer knows about those plots. Representatives from the FBI will be sitting in on our interview with him."

"When do you plan to do this?"

"Tomorrow. Around noon. Can you bring him down to the police station for us?"

"I would be uncomfortable with that."

"Why?"

"It would be a betrayal."

"Okay, if that doesn't work for you, why don't we meet you someplace, and you can just turn him over to us?"

"Like where?"

"You go to Balboa Park a lot. Why don't you make some excuse for going over there with him? You can leave him in the van and tell him you're going inside one of the buildings to get something. While you're in there, we'll quietly arrest him and take him Downtown. You won't even have to watch it happen."

"Balboa Park's a big place. Where do you want to do this?"

"Do you know where Alcazar Garden is?"

"Yes."

"There's a parking lot right behind the garden. Meet me there tomorrow at noon."

• • •

I had barely finished my conversation with Tindal, when the cell-phone rang again. This time it was Ilsa. She was hysterical, barely able to talk.

"Justin," she said, her voice trembling with emotion, "can you come over to the park? I need to talk to you."

"What happened?" I asked. "What's wrong?"

"Just come over here," she pleaded. "I'll meet you by the fountain."

"I'll be right there."

I quickly drove over to Laurel Street, crossed the bridge, and entered Balboa Park. I parked the van in the closest parking lot and jogged the rest of the way over to the fountain. Ilsa was sitting on one of the benches, looking down at the ground, her right hand across her forehead.

"What happened?" I asked as I sat down next to her and placed my arm around her shoulder.

"I was almost killed today," she said, looking up at me. Her eyes were filled with fear.

"How?"

"I took an early break and walked across the Laurel Street Bridge to get a donut and some coffee. As I was crossing Fifth Avenue, a car came racing down the street, coming directly at me. I froze. I couldn't move. I just stood there. Then I felt someone grab me and pull me out of the way. It all happened so fast I couldn't . . ."

Her voice trailed off, and she shuddered as she tried to compose herself.

"You make it sound like the driver of that car was deliberately trying to run you over."

"That's the way it felt. He just raced down the street, probably going fifty, sixty miles an hour. Maybe faster. If someone hadn't pulled me out of the way just in time, I would have . . ."

"Who pulled you out of the way?"

"I don't know. He didn't say anything to me. As soon as he saw that I was safe, he patted me on the shoulder and walked into The Huntress."

"What did he look like?"

"He was stocky, well-built. Looked like he might have once been an athlete. And he wore a baseball cap."

"A New York Yankees baseball cap?"

"I don't know one baseball cap from another. I'm just glad he was crossing the street when that car came bearing down on me. Otherwise, I wouldn't be here talking to you."

• • •

After Ilsa had settled down, I told her Tindal wanted me to turn A. C. over to him the next day. Then I drove over to my apartment and sat in my reading chair while I pondered some of the strange, inexplicable coincidences that seemed in retrospect to fall into an ominous pattern. I remembered A. C.'s very words the previous day, when he had quizzed me on my knowledge of history. He had said, "Most people think it is the big events that shape history. It is not. It is the smallest things imaginable. They are what shape history. A cough, a pause to study a flower, a step to the right instead of to the left—those are the things that shape history. After that, everything on the planet moves in a different direction than it might otherwise have travelled."

Later that same day, while he was looking at the cemetery stone for John Martin Whittier, A. C. made a similar provocative comment when he said, "If this young man here had taken one step backwards, instead of one step forward, it would have changed the world."

Why had he felt compelled to make those comments? Was he anticipating what would happen to Ilsa the very next day?

When I talked to Mac, he insisted that he did not make it to the major leagues because his eyesight deteriorated overnight, and he could no longer pick up the spin on a curve ball. He attributed the deterioration of his eyesight to some men in business suits who had invaded his dreams and told him they had something more important they needed him to do. After that, Mac had to give up on his plans to become a major league baseball player. Instead, he became somewhat of a Laurel Street character who established a daily routine that took him from Jake's Club to The Huntress to the Downtown bars at almost the same times every day. Sid, the bartender at Jake's Club, had said you could almost "set your watch by him." If he hadn't been at Fifth and Laurel at exactly the time Ilsa was crossing the street, she would have been killed.

Was saving her life the "something more important" Mac was destined to do? If so, how did the men who invaded his dreams know this? Had they anticipated this incident was going to happen sometime in the future, and they changed Mac's destiny to be there at precisely the time he was needed to save Ilsa's life?

It sounded bizarre. Yet, the seemingly random coincidences fit together too well to be dismissed as mere idle speculation. Then there were the other questions, the ones that were more important than all the others.

Was that car out of control, or was someone trying to kill Ilsa? Was there someone else who did not want the paths of both Ilsa and Mac to come together at precisely that point in time?

><><><><

When I picked up A. C. later that day, he was waiting in his wheelchair on the sidewalk by the brown and white Victorian home.

"I'll be leaving tomorrow," he said once he was in the van, "and
I won't be back for a long time. I have one more place to visit before
I go. Do you know where Mount Hope Cemetery is?"

"Yes. It's over by Market Street, in one of the poorer sections of
the city."

"Take me there," he insisted. He looked out the side window
and remained silent for a time. Then, in the rearview mirror, I saw
him look back in my direction. "Are you curious about who I was
visiting with today?" he asked.

"Just a little," I admitted.

"She's the wife of John Martin Whittier. She never remarried.
She's lived alone most of her life."

"The soldier who's buried in the Fort Rosecrans National
Cemetery?"

"Yes, him."

"So, you did know him?"

"No, I did not know him. But I wanted her to know he was not
forgotten."

As we approached the gateway entrance to the Mount Hope
Cemetery, he retreated into his silence once more. When we drove
through the cemetery gates, I could see some tall, extravagantly
designed cemetery stones positioned like sentinels along the sloping embankment in what appeared to be the older, western section
of the cemetery. To my left, along a narrow strip of green lawn
covered with beautiful pine trees, more modest, ground-level and
knee-high cemetery stones were covered in pleasant shadows cast
by the trees.

To my right, there were two perpendicular rows of cypress trees
that bordered the cemetery. They looked like the Christmas trees
sold in supermarket parking lots before they are unstrung and allowed to spread their branches. Each tree was secured with ropes
to a ten-foot-tall, wooden pole that restricted any horizontal movement of the branches. The trees looked like they had been deliberately tied to the stakes and deprived of water and nourishment to
keep them from growing into fully developed trees.

On the other side of the two rows of trees, there was an open, weed-strewn area that was barren of any cemetery stones, trees, bushes, flowers, or color of any kind. Dead grass and weeds covered the entire area. The only marker visible from the road was a single knee-high, black, granite stone with a white cross etched on the surface that was positioned in the middle of the dead vegetation. That part of the cemetery sloped gently downwards in a southerly direction that ended with a row of trees that partially concealed some railroad tracks. Shallow indentations of various sizes covered the entire area.

Once we were outside the van, A. C. paused and surveyed the parched, barren section of the cemetery.

"What do you know about this cemetery?" he asked.

"Not much, I'm afraid," I said. "My parish was much farther north."

"Do you know what this part of the cemetery is used for?" he asked.

"No."

"It's the Evergreen Cemetery, better known as Potter's Field," he explained.

"I've heard of it, but I've never been out here," I replied as I surveyed the dead vegetation that covered the unirrigated area. "Evergreen Cemetery seems like kind of a strange name for a place where there isn't a single blade of green grass."

"There are four thousand people buried on these ten acres," A. C. explained. "Most of them had no families, no one to claim their bodies. When they died, they were placed in simple pine boxes and stacked, often two or three deep, in unmarked graves. When some of the boxes collapsed, they created the indentations you see out there now."

"How do you know all of this?" I asked.

"I've been here before," he said.

"When?"

He ignored my question and said, "I've been to many Potter's Fields. . . . Do you know how the name came to designate the place where the poor and homeless are buried?"

"It was associated with Judas's betrayal of Christ and his attempt to give the money back to the priests," I replied.

"Yes, indeed, that is what happened," A. C. agreed. "Judas felt incredible remorse for having betrayed Christ and turning him over to the Roman authorities. When he tried to cleanse his conscience by returning the money to the priests, they refused to take it back because it was considered tainted. Instead, they used it to purchase a plot of land that would become a burial ground for the poor and indigent. It became known as Potter's Field because the previous owner of the land had been a pot maker. Over the centuries, that name came to designate any common burial ground for people too poor to be buried on more respectable soil. This is one of those places."

As A. C. spoke, the cypress trees that bordered the cemetery seemed to be transformed almost immediately in my imagination. I realized they were probably tied tightly to the wooden poles to protect them from the wind, birds, and small animals that might otherwise build nests in their branches. They seemed instead to be symbols of the lost souls that were buried there, never allowed to spread their branches into full, meaningful lives, destined to die alone and forgotten.

A. C. pressed the switch on the armrest and proceeded to navigate the wheelchair through the dead brush and other debris that littered the area until he was in front of the black-granite marker with the white cross. He sat there for several minutes, staring at the cross. Then, with great effort, he managed to push himself to his feet, using the armrests for support.

At first, it looked like he was so weak that he was going to topple backwards into the wheelchair, but he gradually steadied himself, raised his arms, and slowly stretched them above his shoulders. He stood there while a sudden gust of wind flowed through the cemetery, stirring up the dirt and sand into a fine mist that surrounded him. The dead grass and weeds arched in his direction, and the ground around him seemed to ripple as the indentations above the collapsed graves swelled gently upwards. He stood there for what seemed like a very long time. Then he suddenly fell backwards into the wheelchair and collapsed.

I quickly rushed over to the granite marker and repositioned him in the wheelchair. His chest did not appear to be rising and falling, and I thought for a moment that perhaps he had died. Then he slowly opened his eyes and looked out over the dead grass, weeds, and sunbaked soil that covered the graves of the homeless and indigent lost souls buried in Potter's Field.

"Now they know they have not been forgotten," he whispered softly.

• • •

Ilsa was so upset after she was almost run over by the speeding automobile that I invited her to spend the night in my apartment. I offered again to sleep on the floor. We stayed awake for a long time, discussing her close brush with death. Later, I shared my many questions about A. C.

"He's leaving tomorrow," I said. "He claims he won't be back for a long time. It sounded like he's leaving for good."

"Where's he going?"

"He didn't say."

"Are you still planning to turn him over to that detective?"

"I don't know. I saw something today. . . ."

I paused in midsentence and tried to decide how I would describe what I had seen to her.

"What did you see?" she asked.

"It's not easy to describe."

"Try me."

"He asked me to take him to the Mount Hope Cemetery. When he was in the section reserved for the homeless and indigent who are buried there, he stood and raised his arms—and it was like everything in the cemetery was trying to move toward him. I had seen him do it one other time, but not on that scale. It made me realize Joe Wolff might be right when he said A. C. is not of this world."

"So who *do* you think he is?"

"I don't know," I admitted. "This may sound melodramatic, even preposterous. But he seems at times to be almost some kind of Second Coming. The way he fed the homeless with forty or fifty sandwiches he couldn't possibly have stuffed into those small, leather pouches on the sides of his wheelchair. That's almost a modern-day reenactment of one of Christ's miracles in the *New Testament*. The homeless people in his drawing. I only noticed the other day that there were twelve of them. And the dark skin blotches on his head. They look like scars."

"You never said anything about those before."

"I never saw them before. Two days ago, when I picked him up at St. Joseph's Catholic Church, he had his cap off for the first time. The top of his head was scarred and covered with dark blotches. Then there's his busted-up feet, his apartment number 312, and so many other things. They can't all be coincidence. There are biblical references in the *New Testament* for most of them. If I turn him over to Tindal, what does that make me? I feel like something very powerful is pushing me to play the role of Judas in a modern-day version of the crucifixion."

"I think you're reading too much of your training as a priest into all of this," Ilsa gently admonished me. "Coincidences do happen. It doesn't mean they are all part of some otherworldly prophecy to destroy or save the planet. Things often happen that appear to be related, but aren't."

Ilsa's voice grew weaker, and she fell asleep even as we talked. I had too much on my mind to fall asleep so easily. I could not get comfortable on the floor and decided instead to sit in my reading chair to see if that would help me relax. I watched as the moonlight filtered gently through one of the window shades and softly illuminated the bed where Ilsa was sleeping. I watched as her chest rose gently and fell with each quiet, almost imperceptible breath. Seeing her lying in my bed was comforting and reassuring.

Once again, I reviewed the events of that day and wondered if perhaps Ilsa and I had been brought together to fulfill a future role that was, as yet, concealed from both of us. She had come into my life in a most unusual way, seemingly from nowhere. I still knew virtually nothing about her, except that she was born in the east and her ancestors could be traced back to Europe. Other than that, she was almost as much of a mystery as A. C.

Had some powerful, hidden forces thrown us together to fulfill a destiny that neither of us would understand until later in our lives? Had those same forces foreseen that she would be in peril that very day and placed a most improbable guardian angel in her path to save her life?

As I continued to watch Ilsa, I again questioned whether my own destiny had been shaped by similar forces. Perhaps I, too, had been directed down an improbable path that took me out of my church parish and into the small studio apartment where I would someday meet Ilsa.

Is something trying to tell me that my purpose in life is not to be a priest? Is it directing me to a different life I am supposed to live?

My thoughts eventually shifted back to A. C. He had also come into my life unannounced. Somehow, he knew it would be me who was carrying his handwritten note into the foyer the first day we met. Someone else could easily have seen the note and taken it down from the bulletin board, but he knew it was me. He even knew my name.

Why?

I decided some of those answers would probably become clearer to me the very next day, if and when I turned him over to Tindal. It was not what I wanted to do. I preferred to have no part in such a betrayal.

Did Judas feel the same way? Or was Ilsa right, and I was making too much out of what was going to happen the next day at Alcazar Garden?

I put all other thoughts out of my mind and focused instead on Ilsa. For a moment, I was at peace with myself as I watched her chest rising and falling as she slept on my bed, and the soft moonlight filtering through the apartment window settled gently on her sleeping form.

CHAPTER THIRTEEN

The next morning Ilsa decided to take the day off to help me. A. C. was late in joining us by the mailboxes. By the time the elevator doors opened and his wheelchair rolled into the foyer, it was almost eleven o'clock, an hour before I was supposed to deliver him to Tindal. I introduced him to Ilsa, and we left together.

As tired and worn out as A. C. had appeared the previous day, he looked much worse, almost deathlike. His cheeks were sunken and gaunt, as though he had stopped eating, and his skin color was grayish white. He slumped against the armrests on the wheelchair like a man who barely had the energy to sit upright. He didn't even try to make conversation with us until we were in the van. Then he seemed to regain some of his energy, and he sat more erect and looked out the side window.

"Are you taking me to Balboa Park today?" he asked.

"How did you know that?" I said.

"Isn't that the way it always starts?"

"*What* always starts?" I asked.

"The beginning of the end," he replied. "But I need you to take me someplace else first. Tecolote Canyon Natural Park. I want to check on the bees. I need to see how they're doing. Then we'll decide where we will go next."

"I've already been there," Ilsa said. "The bees are not doing well."

"Take me there anyway," A. C. insisted.

I decided to take a circuitous route through Mission Hills, Old Town San Diego, and then over to Morena Boulevard. I took a right on Tecolote Road and drove over to the entrance to the natural preserve.

"This is fine," A. C. said. "Stop here and let me out."

I pulled over to the shoulder of the road and helped him get out of the van. As he drove his wheelchair over to some tall, green bushes off to the side of the road, I got back into the van.

"I was out here just the other day," Ilsa said as she watched A. C.'s wheelchair approach the bushes. "That area over there was covered with dead bees. It looked like something had killed every bee in Tecolote Canyon."

As we watched A. C., he leaned over and picked something up off the ground. He held it in his open palm and seemed to be gazing at it intently, while he prodded it with his other index finger.

"What's he doing?" I asked as a bee flew out of his hand and circled his open palm.

"I don't know," Ilsa said, shaking her head in disbelief.

Suddenly, the cellphone I had stuffed into my shirt pocket that morning began to vibrate and ring. I flipped open the lid and saw Tindal's name on the screen.

"Yes," I said. "What is it?"

"I thought you were meeting me at Alcazar Garden," he said.

"I am."

"Then what are you doing over by Tecolote Canyon? You look like you're going in the opposite direction."

"He wanted to see something over here before I drove him back to Balboa Park."

"Is there anything else I need to know?" Tindal asked.

"No."

"Then I expect you to be here in half an hour," he insisted. "We'll be waiting."

"They know precisely where we are," I said to Ilsa as I closed the cellphone. "I think they suspect we're not going to deliver him to them."

She was so fixated on A. C. that she didn't seem to hear a thing I said to her. She pointed in his direction and said, "Look at that."

There was a huge swarm of bees circling A. C.'s wheelchair. Other bees were leaping off the ground, as though they had been revived from some long slumber and were overjoyed to be spreading their wings and flying once again. A. C. had a soft, gentle smile on his face as he raised his right arm and moved it in a circular motion, while the bees continued to swirl around the wheelchair.

"He's resurrected the whole colony," Ilsa said, her voice trembling, as though she could not believe what she was witnessing. "They were all dead. I saw them lying on the ground. There's no way he could do that. It's not possible."

"He knows what's coming next," I said. "He's giving me an opportunity to do the right thing."

"About what?" Ilsa asked.

"We need to get him to wherever he needs to go!" I said as I rolled down the side window and threw the cellphone into the brush on the side of the road.

"Why did you do that?" she asked.

"Because they're using it to track us."

I watched as A. C. waved his right arm again, and the entire swarm of bees flew into the bushes that covered the area. He watched them for a moment, and then he smiled gently and drove his wheelchair over to us. I quickly secured him in the rear of the van. In the distance, I could hear the faint sound of police sirens.

"Now I'm ready to go," he said as I slipped behind the driver's wheel. "Take me to the Mission Beach Pier."

As I drove out of Tecolote Canyon, the police sirens grew louder and seemed to be converging on the area where we were located.

"They've probably got another tracking device on this van," I said. "Tindal's the type that would leave nothing to chance."

I drove north on Morena Boulevard and turned west onto Garnet Avenue. When I heard still more police sirens ahead of us, I exited Garnet Avenue and drove through several alleys, while I kept moving in a westerly direction. I made more turns onto other side streets and alleys until I was able to pull up to the registration office for the Mission Beach Pier cottages.

I quickly helped A. C. out of the van.

"Is someone picking you up here?" I asked, looking in all directions.

"Yes," he replied. "They will be here."

"Where?"

"They will be waiting for me on the pier."

"You'll be trapped out there."

"Just take me to the end of the pier," he insisted.

Ilsa grabbed one handle on the back of the wheelchair, and I grabbed the other. We pushed as hard as we could and ran behind the wheelchair as the sound of police sirens converging on the pier grew deafening. As we approached one of the blue and white cottages, a bearded figure suddenly stepped out and held his hand out to stop us.

It was Waldo!

He looked every bit as menacing as he had the day he had entered the church rectory and killed his wife.

"It's okay," A. C. said, turning and whispering over his shoulder. "He's with us."

"How can that . . ."

"It's all in my computer," A. C. replied quickly. "I left it for you. The apartment door and the computer are unlocked. . . . You will find what you need to know for now. There is more that will come later."

Waldo suddenly walked around to the rear of the wheelchair, grabbed both handles away from Ilsa and me, and started pushing the wheelchair toward the end of the pier. He covered the remaining distance in powerful, effortless strides.

Ahead of us, a group of well-dressed men and women in business suits stepped out of the cottages on both sides of the pier. They were the same business associates I had seen A. C. meet with on several different occasions. They walked swiftly to the end of the pier and lined up on opposite sides of the boardwalk. Two fishermen, hearing the police sirens and not knowing what was happening, but realizing it was probably something ominous and threatening, leaned their rods against the guardrail and made a quick retreat past us as they ran to the entrance to the pier.

In the distance, a light fog appeared on the horizon and moved slowly in our direction. Behind us, I heard the sound of footsteps on the thick, wooden planks that covered the pier. As we raced onto the observation deck at the very end of the pier, the fog suddenly streaked across the ocean waves and engulfed us. A bright light appeared in the fog and grew increasingly brighter as the men and women in business suits peeled off like a well-trained military unit and stepped into the comforting glow of the light. Each of them became a dark silhouette before disappearing completely. Waldo followed behind them and also disappeared.

Then the homeless masses, apparently from Potter's Field, surged out from the wheelchair and poured into the light in a seemingly endless stream of broken, shattered humanity. They shuffled, stumbled, at times almost fell to their knees before standing again, seemingly held erect by some unseen force that enabled them to walk tall and proud as they stepped into the light. Like the others who entered before them, their dark silhouettes merged with the bright light and vanished. They were followed by countless innocent victims of war and senseless violence, their wounded and broken bodies now fully healed and whole, who surged out of the wheelchair and marched into the light. One young soldier paused, turned, and smiled at A. C., took one step backwards, turned again, and then stepped into the light. After them came the many lost and broken artists who had died in poverty and oblivion without ever touching a human heart or transforming a single human soul. Some carried their poems, their musical compositions, or their drawings as they stepped into the light. Next came the sick and dying, wheelchair-bound children who sat erect, their heads held high and proud, no longer resting on their chests or shoulders, as they too disappeared into the light. The last person to depart was a small, slim figure who stood up from the wheelchair, stretched, raised his arms to shoulder level and gazed at the sky, lowered them again, and strode into the light.

As he too vanished, there was a rush of powerful ocean breezes, and the fog that had enveloped the end of the pier surged back across the waves and disappeared on the horizon. The only thing remaining on the pier was A. C.'s wheelchair. I walked over to it and found his lifeless body slumped against the backrest. I placed my hand on his neck to see if there was a pulse, but there was none.

I became faintly aware of someone standing next to me.

"What did we just see out here?" Tindal asked.

"Something you'll probably never see again," I said, "unless you're very lucky."

• • •

Tindal asked me to sit with him on one of the wooden benches that were spaced along the guardrails. He pulled out his pen and note-book to record my responses to some questions he said he needed to ask me. His voice faded as he glanced at the end of the pier where the ambulance crew was huddled around A. C.'s wheelchair. A long strip of yellow tape was stretched across the entrance to the pier, closing it to cottage guests and visitors. Except for the ambulance crew and Ilsa, who was sitting on a bench near the other guardrail, Tindal and I were alone on the pier. Finally, he seemed to lose interest in recording my responses to his questions. He stuffed his pen and notebook into his jacket pocket and stared at the end of the pier.

"What happened out there?" he asked. "I've never seen the fog come in and retreat so quickly."

"A. C. insisted he wanted us to take him out here," I explained. "Maybe he knew he was a dying man, and this is where he wanted it to end. Maybe he just wanted to look out over the ocean. Do you know yet who he was?"

"He's not Arnold Clark Davis," Tindal said as he lit a cigarette.

"How do you know that?"

"Davis's body, or what was left of it, just washed up on some beach in Florida. It's been positively identified. I just got the news as I was driving over here."

"Do you still think A. C. was posing as Davis?" I asked.

"No. I don't think so. That was just speculation on my part."

"Then who was he?"

Tindal shook his head and didn't answer the question. "There's something else you should know."

"What's that?"

"I was going through the files on the murder you witnessed in your rectory. The woman who was killed had a gun in her purse. Did you know that?"

"No. She kept pulling tissues out of her purse to wipe her eyes and nose. But I never saw a gun."

"You're probably very lucky. You might have been the real target that day."

"Why would her husband—"

"He probably wasn't her husband. We could find no official records on either of them anywhere. No birth certificates, no marriage license—nothing. Whoever he is, he probably saved your life. The next tissue she pulled out of her purse could have been that gun."

"Why wasn't I told any of this earlier?" I asked.

"We never reveal the details of a murder scene," Tindal explained. "We may need them later when questioning suspects to see just how much they know. If they know some of those details, it usually means they committed the crime. In this case, none of it made any sense. It was unlike anything we had ever dealt with before."

We sat in silence for a time, looking down at the cracked and splintered boards that covered the pier.

"Did you ever figure out who was attacking the homeless?" I finally asked.

"Looks like it was mostly street thugs with a grudge against the world," Tindal replied. "Probably taking out their anger against the most vulnerable among us."

"And A. C., what have you learned about him?" I asked.

"Nothing."

"Nothing?"

"We've found no connections to a terrorist organization, drug cartel, art thieves, or any other criminal organization."

As we talked, I heard the sound of wheels rumbling across the wooden planks on the pier. The ambulance crew pushed the gurney carrying A. C.'s sheet-covered body past the area where we were sitting. The only part of A. C.'s body that was visible was his right hand, which had slipped out from underneath the sheet as the gurney rumbled across the wooden planks. The skin on the back of his wrinkled hand was scarred and covered with small, dark age spots.

"Who do you think he was?" Tindal asked as he watched the gurney pass by.

"I still don't know," I said. "He's from someplace none of us has ever been. That's all I know."

"He looks like just another lost, lonely soul," Tindal said in a soft, gentle tone of voice I had never heard him use before. "There seem to be a lot of them out there . . . a lot of them. I don't think we'll ever know who he was."

• • •

Later that afternoon, I made arrangements for a funeral service and burial for A. C. I called Father Timothy and asked him to help me with the details because he had considerable experience breaking through the red tape at the county coroner's office to release the bodies of San Diego's indigent and homeless population. He said he would take care of everything. He also offered to pull some strings with the cemetery where I thought A. C. would have wanted to be buried. Finally, he said he would contact Joe Wolff to see if he could round up the homeless men and women who were in A. C.'s drawing and see if they would be willing to attend a brief graveside service.

The next morning, Ilsa and I drove over to the East Side Rescue Mission. We made a short detour and stopped at the St. Joseph's Catholic Church so I could place A. C.'s wheelchair in the foyer with the other donated items lined up along the wall. I decided A. C. would have wanted it to go to some poor soul who could not afford a wheelchair. I did not go into the interior of the church. I stayed in the foyer and looked down the long aisle to where A. C. had sat for almost eight hours staring at the statue of the crucified Christ.

After I returned to the van, Ilsa and I drove through the Downtown area and over to the rescue mission. Father Timothy met us in the parking lot. He was standing next to the ancient school bus I had earlier seen parked on the side of the mission building.

"Were you able to get everything done?" I asked.

"Yes," Father Timothy replied. "It's all set. The burial has already taken place. Everyone is in the bus, so let's get going."

He climbed into the driver's seat of the bus and shut the door behind him. A huge puff of gray smoke belched out of the rear exhaust when he turned the key in the ignition. Moments later, the bus pulled slowly out of the parking lot and onto the street. Ilsa and I followed closely behind in A. C.'s van.

It was a short trip through the poverty-stricken streets of the east side to the Mount Hope Cemetery. On the way, I explained to Ilsa that Father Timothy had to get special permission to have A. C. buried in Potter's Field because Mount Hope was no longer accepting the bodies of the city's indigent population. Those bodies were being sent to another cemetery south of the city.

When we arrived at Mount Hope, Ilsa and I immediately got out of the van. As we walked over to the bus, the doors suddenly sprang open, and the homeless people I had seen in A. C.'s drawing surged out. It seemed like everyone A. C. had drawn that day had agreed to attend his graveside service.

I had expected they would look beaten and defeated, but they didn't. Instead, they seemed determined to participate in our ceremony in any way they could. The last to depart from the bus was Joe Wolff. He paused and stared across the empty barrenness of Potter's Field.

Almost as one, we walked across the hardened, sunbaked soil and assembled in the very center of the field, near the black cemetery stone with the white cross where A. C. had stood only days earlier. A new grave had already been dug and filled. The gravel and soil that covered it were a slightly darker color than the surrounding area. I knew that in another day or two, the sun would bake away whatever moisture existed in the soil, and A. C.'s grave would disappear into the dead grass and weeds that covered the rest of Potter's Field.

When we were all assembled in a rough circle around the newly filled grave, Father Timothy opened a well-worn Bible and read two passages from the Book of Psalms. Then he spoke extemporaneously, interweaving into his eulogy some of the stories I had told him about A. C.

"None of us ever really knew who this man was," he said, gesturing at A. C.'s grave. "In that respect, he's no different than most of the other men and women who are buried in this part of the cemetery. There are no markers here to memorialize their time on Earth. There were probably very few people, if any, who gathered around their graves when they were lowered into them. I attended some of those graveside ceremonies over the past four decades, and often I was the only one out here. Even the men who dug and filled the graves were gone. So I felt like I had been blessed with a special privilege, for I knew I would probably be the last person to ever acknowledge these poor, lost souls. It was highly unlikely that anyone would ever again stand over their graves and think about them. Indeed, no one would even know where those graves were located. It did not have to be that way, but it was. All of you who were so willing to come here today are a testimonial to how much this person we know only as A. C. meant to you in the brief time that you knew him. I never met him, but through you I sensed that he was more than what he appeared to be. Perhaps when he stood by this very marker and raised his arms, he was gathering these lost souls onto himself. Perhaps he was taking them with him to a place they could truly call home. Life has not been easy for all of you who are assembled here today, or for those underneath the soil we stand on. You have struggled as much as the others who are buried in this Potter's Field. But you do not have to be buried in the most extravagant parts of this cemetery, your name inscribed on an expensive granite or marble stone, for your life to have meaning. If we listen to the words that are so eloquently stated in the *New Testament*, it is the poor who will be welcomed with unconditional love into the Kingdom of Heaven. The rich and famous may have the more beautiful stones in this cemetery, but they may also find it much more difficult than the poor to find a pathway to whatever comes after this world. Whoever we are memorializing today, whatever his real name might be, he seems to have much in common with these other nameless graves that surround him. All of them must never be forgotten."

After Father Timothy concluded his remarks, and the others who had stood around A. C.'s unmarked grave were walking back to the school bus, I remained behind. Before leaving, something told me to look at the other side of the black-granite cemetery stone with the white cross on the front. Much to my surprise, the words, "Never Forgotten," were inscribed at the top of the stone. They seemed to have been placed there for all of the homeless men and women who lay in unmarked graves beneath the soil of Potter's Field—and perhaps for the rest of humanity as well.

• • •

As soon as we returned to our apartment building, Ilsa and I took the elevator up to the third floor. I had decided earlier that I would not tell the manager A. C. had died until Ilsa and I had an opportunity to retrieve his computer and other personal belongings, if he had any.

After we opened the door and stepped into the cool darkness of his apartment, I carried two of the kitchen chairs over to the living room table, and we sat in front of the computer screen. The starburst screensaver disappeared as I typed in the word *Michelangelo*. We waited for the name to appear on the screen in bold, capital letters. Once it appeared, it lingered on the screen for an unusually long time. I was beginning to question whether A. C. had unlocked the computer, when suddenly the name slowly disappeared and was replaced by the single word "Welcome," which also disappeared. The screen quickly filled with strange mathematical equations and hieroglyphs that streaked across the monitor.

"What do you make of this?" I asked Ilsa.

"I don't know," she replied, shaking her head in astonishment.

Above our heads, bright starbursts and celestial lights suddenly appeared on the ceiling. They were soon replaced by rows of numbers organized into columns that accelerated across the ceiling in seemingly random patterns. The ceiling itself became more translucent and glasslike.

"Any idea what those mean?" I asked, pointing at the numbers.

"It seems to be . . . some kind of statistical chart," Ilsa replied.

"Of what?"

"I have no idea."

"Ever see anything like it before?"

"No . . . well, yes, actually. I saw something like this in a statistics class. The professor showed us how to use a software program to organize statistical data. But this is far beyond anything we were ever taught."

"What was the purpose of it?"

"To find a match of some kind between a random set of numbers."

"Did you find it?"

"Yes. But this seems like an infinite set of numbers and possibilities. If it's a search, it must be looking for something extremely rare."

As the numbers faded and disappeared, A. C.'s wheelchair slowly came into view. It was surrounded on all sides by what appeared to be a barren desert somewhere in the Holy Land. A. C. was nowhere in sight, although he narrated from off screen.

"I apologize, Justin, for the way we parted," he said. "I know you probably have many questions you need answered. You deserve those answers because you will play an important role in what comes later. I know you have been concerned about the many unpredictable twists and turns in your life—and you have a right to be. Ilsa and you have had protectors from the day you were born. We have followed you, and in some cases planned ahead for many years to insure your safety. We cannot control the future, but we can nudge it in the direction we hope it will go. I am rather limited, and my role is small, but there are others who are far more powerful. They helped to neutralize the threats to your lives from those who prefer a different future and will stop at nothing to insure that it happens. Someday you will understand why that is the case."

As A. C. narrated, a montage of my life's experiences started to move across the ceiling, followed by a brief montage of some key moments in Ilsa's life. Many of the scenes that played out on the ceiling showed us at the very moments when our lives were in great danger.

"Justin," A. C. continued, "when you did not open your apartment door that night when someone tried to lure you into the hallway, or when a young woman rushed into the rectory and begged for your help—we were there for you. And Ilsa, when you almost drowned when you were a young girl, or when you crossed the street and a speeding car almost ran you over—we were there, too. Yes, sometimes we fail and arrive too late, as was the case with John Martin Whittier, but we always try to protect those we need to fulfill our vision of a different world than the one you now inhabit. Still, our work goes far beyond what I have just shown you. The world is often a frightening and seemingly hopeless place. The masses who inhabit it struggle to find enough to eat or enough clean water to drink. They see their children waste away and starve. Yet most of them do not give up. They continue to participate in the eternal struggle to survive, while others who care little for them will stop at nothing to destroy their spirits so they will accept their hopeless lives without complaint."

As A. C. spoke, a new montage of images flowed across the ceiling. Impoverished men and women in soiled, dirty clothing, and holding signs protesting their working conditions, manned a barricade in front of a smoke-belching factory while security guards armed with clubs and rifles beat them into submission. An exhausted young girl with listless eyes and shattered spirits looked up from a sewing machine in a garment sweatshop. A homeless mother and father with two children, wrapped in plastic garbage bags and clinging to one another for warmth and comfort, huddled together in a small alcove at the top of a concrete staircase of an urban bank building.

"We have also been unable to stop your wars," A. C. continued, "and their subsequent aftermaths that only add to the suffering of the world's impoverished masses. War is the one thing the human race seems to have perfected, while the more pressing moral and ethical issues have atrophied through ignorance and greed. If half the time and resources that are devoted to the world's wars would have instead been devoted to eliminating poverty and disease, the human race would be much farther along in achieving its spiritual mission."

Another montage moved slowly across the ceiling. A series of images appeared of various battlefields after the fighting had ceased, leaving behind the mutilated corpses of hundreds of soldiers, some with their eyes still open, staring at the sky. Another image appeared of children on their hands and knees drinking rancid water that had collected in a shell crater. A final image depicted human skulls piled high in neat rows like merchandise displayed in a warehouse.

"So you see," A. C. continued from off screen, "we must intervene occasionally to manipulate the history of your world, or all will be lost. We did it with Da Vinci, Michelangelo, Francis Bacon, Bruno, Mozart, Einstein, and so many others. We keep trying in the hope that someday one of your kind will lead you out of the eternal madness that engulfs the human race. But we have enemies, some within our own organization. They have other plans. They have a very different view of the future they want to create. Our division has a limited charge and even more limited resources. We are a voice for the poor, but we also explore and inventory the creative potential of the human race. Art is often your greatest achievement. It is what will convince our superiors, if anything can, that the human race deserves to survive. Yet, your artists are often destroyed by those in power who perceive them to be threats. Still, through our efforts, sometimes we succeed in creating a Michelangelo. When we do, we have renewed hope that the human race will rise above its weaknesses and reach for the hand of God, as Michelangelo depicted it on the Sistine ceiling. As Michelangelo understood so well, the universe was created as an act of love."

Michelangelo's painting of *The Creation of Adam* suddenly spread across the ceiling, making it seem like A. C.'s apartment had been instantly transformed into the Sistine Chapel. We found ourselves gazing upwards at the panel in which God reaches out to bestow the gift of life to Adam, while His other arm is draped protectively over Eve. The panel remained on the ceiling for the duration of A. C.'s narrative.

"When great genius comes wrapped in humility," he continued, "it can change the world. Still, those hopes are usually crushed by others at EWE who favor a more hostile approach. They want to eliminate everything and start all over. They have tried just about every way possible to destroy the human race, and they will continue to try to destroy it. Floods, fires, earthquakes, comets—this time it is the bees. For now, suffice it to say that I have just filed my final report. I hope it will satisfy those who favor more drastic actions. I have audited many of your governments, your churches, and your financial institutions. You need better and wiser political and spiritual leaders. They are often hopelessly corrupt, a disgrace to the spiritual and creative forces that govern the universe. There are occasional acts of kindness. But your world and those who control it have been a huge disappointment. They are consumed by greed and self-interest. I thought surely things would have progressed beyond this point. Still, I have made my recommendations. I have informed those who are much more powerful than me that, in my opinion, it is not yet time. I have told them we have not exhausted all options. Hopefully, my recommendations will be honored. However, there is a split at EWE. Sometimes it results in open warfare between those who favor a hostile takeover and those who wish to see the experiment play out to the end. We are among those who want to give it every chance to succeed, preferably through peaceful methods, before other options are implemented. But we are in the minority, and there are less of us all the time who favor that option. We want Ilsa and you in the future. Others do not. We both manipulate events to make our vision for the future come true. There is much ahead of you. Some things you do not yet see coming. Many difficult decisions that must be made. People who will need you more than you know. I must take leave of you now.

I still have much work to do. I do not want End World Enterprises International to render irrevocable judgments before there is a final accounting of what might yet be done to save humanity."

Suddenly, Michelangelo's painting of God reaching out to bestow the gift of life to Adam disappeared, and Ilsa and I were left staring into the eternal darkness that covered the ceiling.

• • •

I don't remember anything that happened for the rest of that evening. It seemed as though something in A. C.'s room stole into my mind and usurped control of my every thought and emotion. I don't remember leaving his apartment and returning to the first floor. I don't remember when Ilsa and I parted company and went our separate ways. I don't remember saying goodnight to Ilsa. The time between the very moment when the screen went black in A. C.'s room and I awoke in my apartment the next morning seemed to follow consecutively upon one another without any interruptions.

When I awoke, I was lying in my bed, on top of the covers, fully clothed. I looked around to see if Ilsa was in the apartment with me, but there was no sign of her. I reached for the pillow next to me and saw that it was crumpled and deeply indented, as though someone else had shared the bed with me the previous evening, but I was now alone.

I quickly got out of bed, glanced at the clock on the nightstand, and saw that it was 10:00 in the morning. How it had gotten to be that late, I did not know. I opened my door and glanced up and down the hallway, but there was no one else around. Then I noticed the door to Ilsa's apartment was slightly ajar, and I pushed on it and watched it swing slowly open. I immediately felt like I was looking into A. C.'s apartment.

There was nothing in the apartment except for a single folding table next to a window at the far end of the room. As I walked into the apartment, I surveyed the adjacent rooms and saw that they, too, were empty of everything except for the barest rudiments of furniture.

It's completely abandoned!

When I walked back into the living room, I spotted a tablet lying on the folding table. When I held it up to the sunlight streaking through the window, I realized it was a note from Ilsa:

Dear Justin,

I hate to leave you like this. I know you deserve a better explanation for why I had to go. I have a new work assignment that will take me much farther north to try to preserve more endangered bee colonies. My sole mission and purpose for existing is to protect the bees. Unfortunately, I must sacrifice everything else to that purpose, even those things others consider far more important in life. We will cross paths again someday. Of that, I am certain, although it will undoubtedly be in a far different place than the two adjacent apartments we have shared.

Much love always!

Ilsa

I did not know what to make of Ilsa's sudden disappearance. Why, I wondered, did she not at least take the time to say good-bye? As I looked around the nearly empty apartment, I had another thought.

Is she one of them, too?

I was totally lost, confused beyond all possible reconciliation. Nearly everything and everyone who had consumed my every waking hour, and often my dreams, for the past several months was gone. I had hoped Ilsa and I could retrace our steps through the imponderable mysteries that had surrounded and nearly destroyed us. I had hoped that more answers might be forthcoming from those who had placed us on our life's paths. I had even considered that someday, perhaps, we might take the same path for whatever years remained. As I looked around the empty apartment, I realized none of that was meant to be.

We had different missions in life. She has found hers. I had yet to find mine.

I finally walked back to my own apartment. I sat down in my reading chair, closed my eyes, and pondered how I was to spend the rest of that day, and the rest of the many days and weeks and months and years after that one. I was reluctant to slip back into my previous life as a reclusive, anti-social hermit struggling with my obsessions. A. C. and Ilsa had awakened in me an overwhelming desire to do something more, albeit I did not know what that "something more" was supposed to be.

I probably fell asleep while I was ruminating about my future and where the years ahead might take me. When I opened my eyes again, I was looking directly at the book I had placed facedown on the end table shortly after Detective Tindal knocked on my apartment door for the first time. After I turned on the reading light, I commenced reading the book where I had left off months earlier.

As I read the chapter on some of the world's great saints, especially Saint Francis, I realized a story is never over until the last word is written. This was certainly the case for Saint Francis in the years after his death, when others wrote about their experiences with him. His life illustrated the axiom that there are endings behind the ending, and they should not be ignored. Otherwise, the story renders itself vulnerable to those who would prefer to avoid the more ambiguous nuances of life, especially a life well lived in spite of enormous pain and suffering.

The section on St. Francis contained much biographical information and some quotes from the venerable saint's own conversations and teachings. I knew some of the details about his life, but much of the information was new to me. I learned that St. Francis had been a successful businessman before he adopted the nomadic existence of Christ. He deliberately impoverished himself, performed miracles like the ones Christ had performed with the loaves of bread, appeared in visions after his death, and continued to interact with humankind in various ways long after his own life had ended.

During these visitations, St. Francis implored his followers and others to view the poor with empathy and compassion. He told them the poor, because they were bereft of all material obstacles that encumbered the wealthy, had a clearer view of the ultimate purpose of life and how it was to be achieved. They were, in the eyes of St. Francis, closer to God than the rich.

Later, the author quoted from the book *The Little Flowers of Saint Francis*. He described a Brother Leo who claimed Saint Francis returned to Earth periodically after his death to attempt to change the course of human history. In one of those visions, Brother Leo said Saint Francis told him, "Oh, Brother Leo, do you remember when I was in the world I predicted that a great famine would come over the whole world, and I said I knew of a certain poor little man for the love of whom God would spare the world and not send the scourge of famine as long as he was alive . . . I was that creature and that poor little man for love of whom God did not send the famine among men. . . ."

The power of those words, as I sat in my studio apartment surrounded by my memories, was overwhelming. It felt like the mist on a rainy day had yielded almost instantaneously to the sunlight, and the small lightbulb glowing in the reading lamp on my nightstand had illuminated the world and exposed its most cherished secrets for all time.

St. Francis of Assisi!

A. C.?

CHAPTER FOURTEEN

Four years passed, and my life continued on its unpredictable course, taking me to places I had never expected to visit. When I crossed one threshold and entered yet another room, it was usually filled with strange, frightening, and sometimes joyful, albeit temporary surprises. Yet that room was only a preliminary to another room, and another room, and another room after that. None of them seemed to be the place I was destined to live out my life, the place where the purpose of my entire existence was directing me.

In his parting words, A. C. indicated that Ilsa and I had been protected from the many threats to our lives for reasons that were beyond our control or understanding. That seemed to be Waldo's role. Perhaps he was one of the warrior angels described in the Bible. Why Ilsa and I had such a menacing presence for a guardian angel, I still did not know. Or maybe it was all in my imagination.

In the years after A. C. died, and whatever part of him survived and vanished into the mist above the Pacific Ocean, I officially resigned as a priest. After what I had experienced, I knew I was unfit for the daily realities of parish life. I realized I would be unable to attend to the minutia and clerical bureaucracy of a priest's life that often overwhelm and supersede his attempts to live a spiritual life. Yet, in many ways, I still remained a priest at heart.

Instead, I went to work as a volunteer for Father Timothy at the East Side Rescue Mission. When I made my decision to leave the priesthood, I remembered his advice that "often what people think is their true calling is only one small step on a much longer journey." After Father Timothy died and was buried in Potter's Field, as he requested, I became the acting director of the mission until someone else who was more qualified could step forward. When another year passed, and no one had stepped forward, I became the new director of the East Side Rescue Mission. I also became the landlord for the homes A. C. had purchased for some of the city's homeless families.

I moved the few things I still possessed into Father Timothy's old office, where I slept on the deeply indented mattress on the cot he had stuffed into one corner of the cluttered room. I lived among donated lamps, boxes of clothing, and other items until they found new homes or were sold to help provide meals and other types of assistance for the homeless population that, in spite of our best efforts, continued to grow and overwhelm the mission.

One of my first decisions as the new director was to hire Joe Wolff as my assistant, and he proved to be amazingly adept at his job. As the weeks and months passed, I felt a certain kinship with the many lost souls who straggled into the mission, stayed a few days to rest and revive their spirits, and then wandered back to the merciless streets. I did not think, however, that the plan for me was to end my life on the east side of Downtown San Diego. I sensed that it involved something more.

What it was, I did not know.

Then, late one summer afternoon when the bees were swarming around the jasmine bushes near the front door of the mission, Joe Wolff walked over to me. He was studying the writing on the side of a small cardboard box.

"Ever seen one of these?" he asked, handing me the box. "Someone left it on that pile over there."

When I pulled a Rubik's Cube out of the box, the red, white, yellow, blue, green, and orange colors were scattered randomly across all six sides.

"I had one of these," I said, twisting it a few times to move the colors to different sides of the cube. "I lost it when I moved my things over here after Father Timothy died. Looks like someone gave up on this one and just decided to get it out of their life."

"I've seen these before," Joe said, chuckling softly to himself. "When I was a boy, I saw some people get pretty frustrated trying to solve them."

"I wasn't able to solve it either," I admitted.

I stuffed the Rubik's Cube into my jacket pocket and walked back into the mission. Inside, I could hear the clanging of pots and pans in the kitchen area. The soft sound of human voices drifted out of the cafeteria where the homeless gathered around our worn banquet tables to enjoy a warm meal while they prepared for another long night on the streets, unless we had enough beds to accommodate all of them.

As I walked down the hallway to my office, I passed a play room Joe had set aside for homeless families with children. Any toys and books that were salvageable from our donations were moved into the room so children who lived on the streets could enjoy some small semblance of a childhood that was only available to children in more secure homes. These children of the streets had never known the simple joy of gathering around a picture puzzle or coloring book with their parents and siblings. We tried to provide some small facsimile of that experience and those simple joys before they had to go back out on the streets.

As I walked past the doorway of the play room, I noticed a mother and her young daughter sitting at one of the children's tables Joe had placed there. The little girl, who appeared to be three or four years old, was studying a coloring book that was open on the table. A box of crayons and some pencils were also spread across the table in front of her.

The mother looked worn and haggard, very much like the other women who came to us for help, except that a quiet, humble attractiveness somehow shone through her dark, stringy hair and dirt-stained cheeks and tired eyes. The little girl, in spite of the poverty that had broken so many youthful spirits who came to the mission, seemed unusually attentive and spirited.

"Are you doing okay?" I asked the mother as I walked into the room.

"Yes," she said, looking up. "Thank you so much for taking us in tonight. We have been sleeping in the park."

"We try to make special arrangements for families with children," I explained. "Even if all of our beds are filled, we try to find something for them."

"Thank you," she said again as her eyes filled with tears. "Thank you so much."

"Are you from this area?" I asked.

"No. We are from much farther north."

"What brought you down here?"

The woman seemed unwilling to answer my question until her young daughter looked up at her and said, "Mama, tell him about the lady who told us we should come here."

"We met a woman who befriended us and gave us the money to come down here," the mother explained reluctantly. "She said there was someone at this mission who she was sure would help us."

"Did she give you her name?" I asked.

"No."

"She's the bee lady," the young girl said, looking up from her coloring book.

"That's what Angie calls her," the mother explained.

"How come?" I asked.

"We met her in a park up there. She became very interested in Angie when Angie showed her some of her drawings. She even gave her a necklace. . . . Angie, show him the necklace the bee lady gave you."

The young girl raised her chin in the air and proudly held up her necklace, which consisted of several small, metal bees attached to a brown shoelace.

"Do you know her?" the mother asked.

"I might," I said as I struggled to keep my emotions in check. I reached into my jacket pocket and placed the Rubik's Cube on the table in front of the young girl. "When you get tired of coloring, you can play with this."

I quickly excused myself and walked back to the office/bedroom I had inherited from Father Timothy. Once I shut the door behind me, I felt a rush of old memories and emotions fill the cluttered room where I struggled to keep the rescue mission afloat financially, and where I occasionally went to be alone with my thoughts.

I was convinced the mother and her young daughter had encountered Ilsa. There was no one else who would have sent them my way.

But how did Ilsa even know I was now running the rescue mission? Did she sense that was the direction my life was taking me? Was that why she left?

Years earlier, I had placed a small, padded kneeler in one corner of the cluttered room, and I had attached a wooden cross on the wall above it. Some nights when I was still trying to make sense of the path my life had taken me, I would kneel in that corner and recite the prayers I remembered from my days as a parish priest. Usually, I went there to deal with some spiritual crisis I could not resolve while I was surrounded by the shattered wreckage of humanity who sought refuge at the mission. This time I knelt there to try to understand some deeply personal, emotional issues that never went away, no matter how hard I tried to make them disappear.

I must have knelt there for a long time because when I stood and looked out the window it was dark, and a welcome silence had settled over the otherwise noisy alley that ran behind the mission.

Before settling into my cot for the night, I decided to pay a quick visit to the large room where we housed the homeless who stayed with us. I wanted to make sure the mother and her young daughter had been assigned a bed and were not forced to sleep on the floor, as was often the case when we had more homeless than we could possibly accommodate.

I walked down the hallway to the room where the cots were spaced in three long rows with two center aisles. Small, green lights glowed on the walls so anyone who got up in the middle of the night would not stumble over any of the other beds on their way to the rest rooms. I found Angie and her mother asleep on a cot near one of those green lights. The soft glow of the light illuminated the mother and daughter as they slept together on the narrow cot. The mother had her arm around the young girl, as though instinctively protecting her child from the darkness just outside the mission walls.

I stood there for a long time, watching the mother and her young daughter sleeping peacefully. I knew for them, as for so many others, this was a welcome respite from the many cold, bitter nights when they had to sleep in bushes or underneath bridges that offered only a little protection from the winds. Beneath the glow of the nightlight, Angie's mother reminded me somewhat of the way Ilsa had looked as she slept on my bed the nights she stayed in my apartment.

On those nights, I stayed awake and watched Ilsa's sleeping form illuminated by the soft moonlight filtering through the window. The moonlight had made her body seem subtly evanescent, almost cloaked in a warm, protective shield. I found myself thinking the same thoughts again as I watched the mother and child who were sleeping on the cot. I struggled with the realization that we could only keep them for a few days, and then we would have to open up new slots at the mission for others who desperately needed to get off the streets—if only for a brief respite from the cold and the hunger.

How can I send them back after what Ilsa—if it was indeed Ilsa—had told them they would find at the mission?

I decided I would see if I could find some small job the mother could do around the mission, maybe in the kitchen, so they could stay longer. Maybe I was playing favorites, but I felt it was something I owed to Ilsa, and perhaps to myself.

Before returning to my bedroom at the other end of the hall, I saw that a light was still on in the play room. We had a policy that all lights, except for the nightlights, had to be turned off before bedtime. Every dime we saved on electricity meant another dime could be used for our meal program. So I decided to turn off the lights in the play area before retiring to bed.

As I suspected, there was no one in the play room, so the overhead lights were serving no useful purpose. I reached for the light switch on the wall and was about to press it downwards, when I saw that Angie's coloring book and the Rubik's Cube were still on the table where she had been playing with them. I decided to bring them back to my room for the night so no one would take them or inadvertently toss them on the donated piles that sometimes littered the hallways.

When I walked over to retrieve them, I saw that the Rubik's Cube no longer looked the way it did when I had placed it on the table. The colors, which had been scattered randomly across all six sides, were neatly organized so all of the red, blue, white, green, yellow, and orange colored squares were on the same sides.

The puzzle was solved.

The coloring book was facedown on the table. When I picked it up and turned it over, I saw that Angie had drawn a picture of a woman in an almost saintly pose with a circular halo of bees hovering around the top of her head. The drawing was so perfectly executed, with flawless attention to details, that it looked like it came from the hand and trained eye of one of the Renaissance masters. The only difference between the Ilsa I knew and the Ilsa the young girl had drawn in the coloring book was that hers looked more like one of the ethereal, spiritualized figures in a Michelangelo painting.

Angie had also given the drawing a title. She had printed the words, "The Bee Lady," across the top of the page. At the very bottom of the page, she had printed her own first and middle names.

Angelina Christine!

POSTSCRIPT

An unexpected knock on the door. A new life, a death, a chance meeting with someone—every motion in the universe is counterbalanced somewhere else. It might not even be on this planet. It might be on the other side of some distant constellation in the darkest recesses of space. Whenever we comfort or ignore the least among us, we change the universe—and nothing is ever the same again.

The original followers of St. Francis recorded his conversations and teachings in many different versions of *The Flowers of Saint Francis*. The specific source for the quotation at the end of Chapter 13 in this novel is Regis J. Armstrong, O.F.M. *Francis of Assisi: Early Documents,* Volume III. (New York City Press: New York, 2001), 512.

ABOUT THE AUTHOR

Dennis M. Clausen grew up in west-central Minnesota near the South Dakota border. There, he gained a close, intimate knowledge of the small towns and the lives they harbored. They provided the inspiration for *The Search for Judd McCarthy*, a best-selling paperback novel published under a different title in 1982. The novel has been republished by Sunbury Press's Brown Posey Imprint (2018). *The Sins of Rachel Sims* (2018), another novel, is the story of a young woman who was reduced to the status of indentured servitude by an extremist religious cult. *The Accountant's Apprentice* (2018), a novel that explores mysterious events that occurred in San Diego in the mid-2010s, is his first novel that takes place in an urban setting. *My Christmas Attic* (2018), the story of a young boy in the early 1950s who struggles with dyslexia and the loss of his father in the Korean War, is set in the mountain town of Julian, California. Clausen is also the author of *Prairie Son* (1999), a book that was the winner of Mid-List Press's "1997 First Series: Creative Nonfiction Award." This book recreates his father's struggles as an adopted child to survive the Great Depression. *Goodbye to Main Street* (2016), a memoir and sequel to *Prairie Son*, explores the many ways past generations impacted Clausen's family history. In addition to his creative work, Clausen has authored textbooks, including *Screenwriting and Literature* (2009), which examines the relationships between writing screenplays and writing novels. For over thirty years, he has taught literature and screenwriting courses at the University of San Diego.